Rites of Passion

Choice of Masters

Thomas has led his life according to the tenets of chivalry laid out by King Arthur. Now his deepest desires and his unshakable honor have joined in single purpose. His soul mate, Lilith, whom he has met only in dreams, is bespelled by a wizard. For five years she has been forced to exist as Lord Zorac's prisoner in a state of high arousal, unable to gain fulfillment.

To free her from her torment, Thomas must perform the sensual Rite of Awakening and convince Lilith to accept his word and hand as that of her true Master. But Lilith's punishment is more than the capricious act of an evil wizard, and all is not as it seems...

Threads of Faith

Marisa is a modern day witch, living at the edge of the woods and at the edge of society, dispensing potions to help lonely souls find their true loves. Because of her inability to live among others, she doesn't believe love is for her, let alone sexual fulfillment. She gets both when Conlon Maguire shows up at her cottage.

He wants a potion to win the heart of his true love, but the magic behind the potion sets its price. The price set on Conlon's potion is that he must spend one night with Marisa, bringing her pleasure. As a servant of the Light, Marisa cannot refuse the price if Conlon agrees to it, but from the moment he touches her, she knows her heart and shields are in danger. How can she go through with it, knowing he will leave her at dawn to be with another?

ISBN: 978-1-942122-46-3

Choice of Masters

A Paranormal Erotic Romance Novella

Joey W. Hill

Chapter One

"By the Holy Mother—"

"For shame, Sir Thomas," the priestess chuckled, her voice as seductive a pull on his cock as the acolyte kneeling before him, sucking on it. "Blaspheming the Virgin's name."

He jerked, his powerful muscles flexing as his grip tightened on the arms of the wooden chair. The rough surface digging into his palms was no distraction from the warm, relentless heat and wetness of the mouth serving him.

The young woman kneeling before his feet was all he could desire. Small, elegant, pure. The priestess had told him she was a virgin, and she was sucking a man's rod for the very first time, those dainty lips never before stretched by a man's brutal need. Her blue eyes lifted to his, reflecting joy in each groan she wrung out of him. Innocence and carnal seduction. The priestess had found his every weakness.

"My lord, you have taken your eyes from her again."

He grunted. Sweat ran down his broad back as he fought for control. He lowered his gaze to the sprite. She balanced herself with a graceful hand gripping his thigh. He started to tremble, gritting his teeth.

"Watch her soft, moist lips pull on your shaft. You have a thick and powerful staff, my lord. It tickles the back of her delicate throat, and stretches her lips so wide she will never smile again without thinking of you. See how she sucks you in, so slow. Hear the noises she makes, feel the glide of her tongue on the underside of your cock."

He moaned, a plea or threat, and his fingers clenched into fists, pulling against the chair. That was the wrong thing to do, because it created a resistance the girl was not expecting. Her tiny mouth slithered down his cock like a thin velvet glove pulling away.

"Celeste, slide your gown up to your waist, and fasten the train so our visitor is able to see the outline of your pretty round bottom. Sir Thomas, don't make me tell you again to keep your eyes on her."

The priestess's fingers grazed his back, using her nails. Thomas's testicles tightened in pleasure at her touch. He looked down as Celeste braced one hand on the floor, and gathered up the train of her gown in the other. She kept on his cock, working it in her mouth, her tongue performing slow, tiny licks, head and body rocking like a lamb suckling its mother's teat. The gown was adjusted and he saw the shape of a perfect white arse, and the fragile bumps of her spinal column. Sweet Christ, the girl didn't even have any scars to mar her perfect skin. Her soft buttocks quivered as she renewed her pumping motion on his organ.

He could do this. He would not go over. He tried to find the sharp edge of that cliff in the passionate haze of his subconscious. He needed to achieve stasis there, give himself more time to understand what thoughts and emotions assaulted a person on the verge of cataclysmic sensation. The High Priestess Helene had dedicated herself to teaching him that control, for nearly thirty days now.

He was far from the man he had been when he entered the doors of this temple. Followers of the Old Way, these priestesses drew their considerable powers from carnal pleasures. No Christian priest or monk dared come near the place, for fear of being ensnared by the sensual delights that were promised behind these walls.

Thomas had thought he understood the sins of the flesh. He had come here for help, but a detached help was what he had wanted. A set of simple instructions that answered his questions and would allow him to be on his way, his contempt toward willfully unchaste women, masked as self-righteous courtesy, intact.

§

He had been brought to Helene's chamber, the High Priestess of Ashteroth. She sat in a chair, regal as a queen, wearing a sheer tunic that showed him her full breasts through its fine sheen. Her nipples were rouged to a dark red, and the down between her legs was as raven black as her hair.

"You seek to free Lilith," she said, in soft tones that slid down his spine, arousing and soothing, evoking a peculiar image of whore and mother at once.

He snapped his spine straight inside his armor, shoving the thought away with anger for his weakness.

He made a bow. "Yes, m'lady. You know the nature of the spell laid upon her, as do we all. I am pledged to rescue her, but I must know how it can be done. It has come to me, through fasting and penance, that you have the information I seek."

"I dreamed of you, too, beautiful man," she said, "and knew you would be coming to ask this of me. But why do you pledge yourself to this quest? Do you seek the glory of defeating a mighty wizard, and earning your spot at an imaginary Round Table that has not existed for centuries, if it ever did?"

Thomas flushed. "You know nothing of my mind."

"To know your mind, I need only watch your cock. It points to her. It is her you want. You want her to call you Master, and yet you want to cherish her with your soul and body. You lie to yourself about your own reasons. I will not help you."

She rose and the woman who had escorted him moved forward to lead him from the temple.

"No," he said. "No."

Helene stepped down from her throne, and passed him, her expression indifferent. The diaphanous cloth of her robe slid along the calf of his armor. It did not catch on the joints, as he would have expected it to do. It moved over him like the wind, like her. Able to touch him with a welcome cool breeze in the cruelest heat, or blast him without mercy. His desperation rose in him, and he spun around as she reached the stone archway.

"No!"

Helene stopped, looked back at him, and said nothing. She gazed at him out of violet gray eyes, so pale he thought of clouds on a day when the sun and rain warred for dominance.

"I dream of her. Nearly every night now, she is there." Thomas took a deep breath, assuaging the pain in his chest. "I pray for your mercy, Lady. You must help me."

§

His dreams of Lilith were vivid, and seemed longer than the night itself, as if time stopped while he was with her. He yearned for his nightly plunge into unconsciousness.

It would start in darkness. He would first be aware of her perfume. She was the flower with an elusive scent, that bud or blossom unseen by a knight traveling through the deep forest. It touched his nose with a haunting fragrance meant to be experienced only a moment, and remembered forever.

Her hair would brush his arm. He would realize that he was standing in this world of darkness in nothing but the flesh God had given him. Her hair was so long that, as she passed, the strands slid over his forearm, feathered across his ribcage, caressed his hip.

He reached out, closed his hand on it. It was like the mane of a steed in a king's stable, so lustrous in weight and health he could feel its beauty through his fingertips. He curled his fist in it and tightened his grip, capturing her. He felt how much stronger he was, how delicate and female she was. She turned into him, rolled herself up against his body in a motion like a languorous summer afternoon. There was a meeting of bare skin. Her slender feet stood on his, her toes stretching to give her extra height. Her hands settled on his shoulders for balance.

Hours of practice had made his shoulders broad and strong, and battle had given them scars. No woman's hand had ever felt this good upon him, not his first tumble, not even the gentle touch of his mother. It was a touch that held everything he wanted, everything he wanted to prove, everything that made him who he was. It almost brought him to tears, and surely the taste of salt on one's lips was not usual in a dream.

Her thighs slid down either side of his erect lance, her heat anointing him with a dew as rich as honey. She was ready for a man, ready for him.

She trembled, and he felt the quiver of her breasts, nipples swollen and tight against the coarse brown hair of his chest. His cock had hardened to an impossible rigidity, rivaling the steel of his sword. His staff bumped up between her legs, the length pressed against her cunt, the ridged head rubbing in the sensitive channel of her arse just beyond the seam of her thighs. Her breathing was rapid, her fingers clutched on his shoulders. He put his hand up and spread his fingers so he covered the side of her neck and cheek, pressing her head to his chest. The pose was as intimate as it was carnal, and he longed to possess her in ways that went far beyond the couplings of flesh.

"Protect me," she whispered into his heart. "Help me. Come to me, my lord. Make me yours."

Moonlight filtered into the dream, bringing light. He looked down at the auburn silk wrapped around his hand, his tether holding her to him. He wanted to see her face. He tugged her head back and the spiral of sensation in his gut tightened in pain and lust at once.

Looking upon her countenance brought him the humility and stillness of a sacred moment, and yet he was harder than he had ever been in his life. He ached to have his hands on her breasts, to bend her over and thrust his cock into the slippery mystery of her womb, making her his, and his alone. He wanted to be all things to her, lover, husband, lord, God to her Goddess. Protector, comforter, seducer.

God help him, he should throw himself to the cold floor of a church to beg forgiveness for the unforgivable sacrilege of such thoughts.

Instead his hands were on her bare waist, his fingers spreading and sliding forward to take hold of her arse. He squeezed the two halves, one in each palm.

"I will always protect you, cherish you, love you," he muttered. "Always."

Her lips parted, lips he wanted to kiss, bite and suck, and from which he wished to bring helpless moans, just as he wished to bring forth a helpless gushing from between her legs.

"Tell me you will be my lady," he demanded.

"I am," she said. "Why else would I be in your dreams?"

The long hair waved around a face as fragile and strokable as the newly opened petals of a white rose. Lips, soft and pink, a bit moist, so that he could not help but think of that other place, just as inviting to kiss with its musky mysteries.

Her eyes were a dark liquid brown like a forest animal. He thought if he lost himself in those eyes, wrapped himself in that auburn hair, it would be like being in the earth, surrounded by her, cradled by her, her child and consort all at once. It was a dream, and he could not stop such pagan thoughts.

Her hands rose to his face, and he kissed her palm, kissed both her palms, kissed every tear from her face.

"Make me yours, my lord," she whispered, her hands sliding to his neck, her body closing in on his.

He lifted her and she gasped as she sunk to the hilt of his jutting cock. It was like being swallowed by velvet and heat, those lips parting to let him in. He felt her contract as she slid down, accommodating his size with shuddering ripples.

Suddenly, instead of being naked, he wore full battle armor, scarred and nicked. His loins were bare, his cock free and erect, and buried in her as before.

She was sweet oil inside, and his rod thickened and lengthened inside her as she rode him. The pump of her hips upon him was as relentless as the stride of his stallion beneath his weight.

"You must bring me, my lord," she rasped, her fingers tightening on his neck, cutting herself on the collar of his armor. "You want to, you have never wanted anything so much as to bugger me."

Thomas reared back to see her face. Her eyes were wild and teeth bared. Her hair came forward in snarled tangles with each stroke to hide her face from him, as if her hair curtained her soul from his scrutiny.

"Lilith, stop." Each upward stroke smacked the vulnerable curve of her stomach against the base of his armor, wounding her flesh.

"No, my lady, do not—" he cried. He tried to stop her motions by banding his arms around her, but she squirmed and her slick cunt milked him, driving him higher. Blood, her blood, was running down his testicles and his thighs. She was screaming in anguish, but she would not stop, and he could not stop her, or himself.

His seed exploded into her body as she wailed in pain, her face a horrifying mixture of lust lost to the madness of suffering, each emotion struggling for dominance. He could not get her to release him. Her legs bound tight around him, her hands gripping his armor as she stared at him with feral eyes. A drop of blood slid from her bitten lip and splashed on the top of her breast.

He awoke, shuddering, covered in cold sweat and his own semen.

§

"The priest recommended prayer vigils, fasting, flagellation, hairshirt, penance in all shapes and forms." Thomas managed to bring his voice back to an even pitch. The priestess stood, still expressionless, her attendant a shadow at her elbow.

"All of this I tried, because he said she was a demon to be cast out. But it makes her so sad. She cries in my dreams when I try to shut her out, when I treat her this way. I know I will do anything to make her smile, to make her mine. It is not what I have known chivalry to be, this wish to possess her, and yet it is. I want to be her Master, yet I also want to be her protector. My soul is torn between lust and devotion and I am going mad."

Helene remained silent. Thomas bared his soul further, casting aside his earlier strategy to hold himself aloof.

"No knight has undertaken the quest to rescue her. They wish the glory of taking from the wizard what is his, but they care naught for her. They see her as his minion and so the prize is not great enough to tempt them. I must help her. I cannot fail, or I shall die at the thought of failing her. Will you help me or not?"

This last, more belligerent than he intended, but he was angry that she had drawn it from him, with her steady stare and calm acceptance of his story that he could not match.

"You do not know if the girl prefers mutton to fowl, if she worries more about our borders or the ribbons she will wear from day to day in her hair. If she is educated, or a simpering fool." Helene raised a brow. "These are important things, my lord."

"It does not matter. In my dream, I know her. She is part of me. I will love her, no matter what she is, or what she is not."

"A man of great discipline, torn between his doubt and what he knows in his heart." Helene pursed her lips. "Yes. I will help you. You are not a true liar." A corner of her mouth twitched. "You were just lying to me, not to yourself. You must stay with me a month to know the way to go about it. Longer, if you can."

"I cannot stay a month."

"It must be a month, or nothing. You obey me in all things for that month, and learn the control you must possess to save her. You will need every moment. You have much armor to shed, Sir Thomas."

§

So here he was, while an innocent licked him with the flames of hell in her tongue. He was stripped of all his clothes, as well as his armor. He had not worn clothes for most of these four weeks. He had walked among the dressed priestesses this way, open to their admiring glances and caresses, as they tested his resolve and his flesh in ways he could not have imagined.

He kept his attention upon Celeste as the priestess had commanded, knowing it would finish him to see the small head bobbing, the soft line of her cheek, the tender wrinkle of her lips as she handled his cock. Still he hoped. He fought it. He tried to think of the cold flagstones of a church in the dead of winter, the scourge taking flesh off his back.

Thomas snarled as Celeste's teeth lightly scored his engorged head. She started making wet, slurping noises of enjoyment, underscoring every lash of her tongue and slide of her lips on him, as if his nerve endings needed the additional help of his hearing to increase his agony.

Her tongue flicked, once, twice, three times along the slender vein that pulsed from scrotum to head, and the vision of scourge and flagstones was consumed by a purifying fire that roared over and through him.

He groaned, the guttural cry of a wild male animal, and he bucked hard, stretching that dainty mouth, plunging into her, wanting her to take all of him deep within her, knowing it was beyond her capacity and not caring. He would bruise her if he needed to, mark her with his power.

He felt the back of her throat and was surprised she did not gag, only lifted her small hands and dug her fingers into his arse, pressing him in further. The mewling noise she made vibrated along his throbbing head.

She took every drop of him. As he emptied, her touch eased and soothed his shuddering skin. As his seed drained, so did his passion, and he stared down at her, filled with shame and fury at himself. She looked up at him, innocent as a doe, and wiped her mouth with the back of her hand, not like a fishwife, but a deliberate movement, as if she was handling a sacrament.

"Leave us, Celeste."

The young woman rose, readjusting her gown and rebelting it. She curtsied to Thomas and her lady, and left them as ordered.

His knees were weak, and it further humiliated him that he could not stand in courtesy to the priestess as he should at this moment. Helene slid a hip onto the arm of the chair, and put a gentle hand on his shoulder.

"You did well that time," Helene said in a neutral voice. "Three hours and the mouths of four of my priestesses to bring forth your seed. Your physical discipline is commendable, Sir Thomas."

He laid his head back and closed his eyes. "Now, who is the liar?" Her fingers stroked his hair, the color of burnished copper, away from his sweaty neck. "I continue to fail."

"No, not in the sense you think. Your physical discipline is perfect, Sir Thomas."

"And yet my body betrays me. Why?"

"My lord," she admonished, "this is not sword fighting, or breaking a lance. Has it ever occurred to you that the secret is not clenching your fist, but opening your fingers and marveling at the shape of your hand, made so by no will of your own?"

"Damn it all, woman, do you always talk in riddles?"

Her low chuckle warmed him, despite his weariness.

"This is a spiritual test for you, my lord, not a physical one." Her violet-gray eyes were serious. "It has been a long life for you," she said. "Has it not? Longer than the years of your face reveal."

He closed his eyes, not denying the truth that burned in his throat to hear it spoken.

Her voice was a mist in his mind. "You are a long way from the time of Arthur, and yet you have served his ideals well. You have forgotten what magic is, because you are tired." She hesitated. "And so lonely."

"I wanted the way to free her to be a way without magic."

"Ah, my lord, you must realize that the power of the body's response, it is a magic all of its own. When the heart becomes involved, it is potent. It is in fact the most real thing on this earth, and the joining of bodies can render all other magics insignificant."

"I saw Lilith once, when she was a young girl in her uncle's court," he admitted. "I did not feel this way about her then. Now she invades my dreams as the grown woman I have never seen, and it is as if I will be unable to breathe if I try to contemplate a life without her in it. I would call it sorcery, but it is not. I have seen enough to know the difference. It is something my heart hungers for as much as my mind."

The priestess's hand traced his damp forehead. "The gods who know our destinies are sometimes kind, sometimes cruel," she clicked a nail over one of the scratches she had made on his back. "Soul mates may pass each other, strangers in this life. It is not time for them to join. In another life, one will recognize the connection and the other will not, leading to heartache. The gods know why, but there are painful lessons we all must learn to achieve our destiny.

"Then," she continued, "there is the blessed life, when they are aware of each other. Suddenly what each feels so deeply in his or her heart is enhanced beyond their imaginings by feeling it together."

"Will she, do you think - "

"I cannot say, Thomas." She tugged on his hair. "I tested your body not only to reacquaint you with sensual pleasures, but to help you understand what it is to hover in that moment where control and the bliss of oblivion are equally beyond your reach. Suspended pleasure is excruciating in its intensity. To decide to stay there of your own volition requires perfect love and perfect trust of the one asking it of you. It is a pleasure of its own.

"However," her expression darkened, "to be forced to stay there is a cruelty beyond measure, because you are completely vulnerable, your spirit as well as your body. Can you imagine feeling like that for five years, Sir Thomas? Everything laid bare, like an animal skinned alive, exposing the complex wonder created by God and Goddess, but unable to bear even the touch of the air? That has been Lilith's life."

He swallowed, the muscles tensing in his shoulders as if he could draw a weapon and spare his lady that suffering. Helene's hand touched him.

"In her dreams, she knows you, and that, I will venture to say, is a good sign. The ritual I will show you will let her reach through the horror of her current existence, pull the curtain back and see you clearly. From there, the choice is hers. If she turns away, out of fear or denial, then you will have lost her in this life. I know Zorac's power, and there is none to equal him, save the Lord and Lady Themselves, or the Christian God, whichever face you prefer to give Divinity. Love is the closest kin to Divinity, so only the pull of a soul mate can wrest her from Zorac's grasp."

"A soul mate she has never met," he murmured.

"But a soul mate nevertheless," she reminded him. "Whether or not you have ever met in this life does not matter, not if the connection is a true one." She molded her hand over his slick shoulder, leaned forward so her breasts pressed against his bare arm, and laid her cool cheek against his. It was a touch of comfort, and power, and he sat still beneath it. "You are a strong man, Thomas. Lilith will respond to the hand of the man who has her heart. You are her Master."

"Will she acknowledge it from the beginning, you think?"

"No. She will be more like the nightmare part of your dream. The wizard has corrupted that within her which is sacred. Her ability to express her love with her body, enjoy her body, and choose to submit to a Master, the man she loves."

He grimaced and turned his face away, but she caught his jaw, made him look into her stern violet eyes.

"You must accept the duality of your nature. You can love Lilith, protect her, and still want to push her to her back, spread her thighs and conquer her. Lust and love together is not a sin, because one balances the other. You are a strong, virile man, a forceful one, and by all appearances," she smiled, "a very determined one. You may love a woman, but you will also want to dominate her physically, have her acknowledge that dominance, submit to you. That is part of your nature. It does not lessen your regard for her. The difference between you and the wizard is you want to win your lady's favor, her desire for you to be her Master, not take that choice from her."

"I was not fair to you, when I came here," he said at last.

"I have grown more attached to you as well, Sir Thomas," her eyes crinkled. "So." She settled back. "I am not what you thought I was. Experience can change the scope of your morality. It can make that scope greater, and, at the same time, focus you on what the most important moral principles are. There are actually only a very few, but they are so important, the fate of every soul rests upon them."

Lilith's fate. It lay unsaid between them.

"Arthur once said,..." Thomas hesitated. The priestess looked at him with that opaque gaze she had mastered. "...To love someone with all your heart, you must believe in her strength and be there at that moment she needs you most, no matter your own fears or weaknesses. Magic, he said, lies in this unconditional gift. At least," he added, shifting, "it is believed he said that."

"You do remember some things," she said softly, a smile crossing her face.

"In my dreams, I remember everything," he said. Exhaustion closed his eyes again, giving him the temporary peace of darkness. "The nightmare as well as the beauty. Like him, all I want now is to hold the woman I love in my arms and know peace."

She smiled. "You have discovered the greatest miracle, in a world of many miracles."

He nodded, and found the strength to raise her hand to his lips. "It is the only one I seek now."

Chapter Two

When the moon rose full in the sky, he took his leave of the women of Ashteroth. He hoped he had the weapons he needed to succeed in his task. He was certain he would give all his strength, his life if necessary. He could tarry no longer with the priestesses, no matter the value of their counsel. He was driven by the call of a dream, the woman of his dreams, who had captured his soul in a way more powerful than sorcery, and who needed him.

A week later, Thomas reined in his horse on the rise just below Zorac's castle. His palms beneath his gauntlets were sweating, and his heart pounded hard against his chest, like a sword relentlessly striking the breast plate of his armor during a battle.

It was not Zorac making him feel thus. Surprisingly, and perhaps foolishly, he felt no anxiety about the wizard. His reaction was all about Lilith. What would she think of him? Would he measure up to her expectations, would he be equal to the task of rescuing her? He prayed it was so. A knight's faith was what saw him through every fight, and he would not shirk it here.

He spurred his mount forward, and the powerful stallion responded, cantering up the approach.

He had spoken to the tenants of the wizard's lands as he traveled across them, and found people who were well fed and protected from harm, content with their overlord. As a soldier, he assessed the castle before him. It was a sturdy structure with walls eight feet high, a gatehouse and round towers. However, its lord apparently relied on magic wardings to protect his holdings. The drawbridge was lowered to allow crossings over a purely decorative sparkling brook, versus a stagnant moat or steep ditch, and the portcullis was open.

There were only shadows to indicate the movement of a few retainers along the curtain walls. The horse snorted at the unusual quiet, his hooves clopping across the boards of the drawbridge. Thomas raised his gaze and brought his mount to a halt several strides back from the portcullis. A man stood on the wall above it.

Thomas twitched the reins on the horse's neck. The horse bent a leg forward and Thomas matched the motion by dipping his own head.

"Greetings, Lord Zorac," Sir Thomas said.

He had no doubt this was the wizard overlord of this place, though it surprised Thomas to see him there, meeting him alone.

The knight had no preconceptions about wizards. He had seen them in many forms. However, Zorac had the bearing of a king. Tall and broad-shouldered like a knight, with golden hair past his shoulders. He was clean-shaven, like Thomas, and his eyes were a transparent pale blue, like water. Despite a handsome mien, he did not appear to be a vain man. His hair was combed and held back with two braided outer strands. He eschewed colors and wore a dark tunic of fine wool with silver trim at the hem, matching dark hose and a fine woven cloak. The right shoulder of the cloak bore an embroidered representation of the crescent moon and a cluster of stars.

Thomas studied the man's face. That Zorac had great power, he knew. He looked for evidence of danger, the tell tale sign of friend or foe, and found it in the wizard's lips. They were thin, sensual, and had a tension to them that suggested his ability to be cruel.

"Greetings to you, noble knight," the wizard replied in a tone that was no more than courteous. "What brings you to my domain?"

Thomas straightened from the bow. "I bring you greetings and regards from the High Priestess Helene, and a challenge from myself."

"The one gains you entrance, and the other piques my

interest," the wizard replied, his attention moving carefully over every aspect of Thomas's appearance. "You wear mail. Have the roads to my home become so dangerous?"

"Nay, my lord." Thomas looked down at his hauberk. "A knight is always prepared to defend the honor of the innocent."

"Or the not-so-innocent." Zorac cocked his head at Thomas's sudden still expression. "The wind carries many tales to me, Sir Thomas. I have some knowledge of why you are here. It will amuse me to hear why you waste your time. Come in and share my table, and your challenge."

Thomas inclined his head. "My lord."

He passed under the grate into the gatehouse and a stable lad was there in the open courtyard to take his horse. The boy put his hand on the horse's neck. "I shall take good care of him, my lord. Does he have any special needs?"

Thomas dismounted. "He's ridden far. Just see he's groomed and well fed and given a dry stall. I'm sure he'd appreciate any further coddling you're willing to give to him."

The boy smiled. One eye was closed, the other gone, the mark of the weapon that had taken it making a diagonal scar from his forehead to his cheek. "Aye, my lord," he said.

"What happened to your face, boy?"

"Raids on the border, my lord. My family was killed and Lord Zorac took me in. He said losing my sight was a small matter, because at times it is best if you do not see too much of this world."

"My lord?"

His heart leaped into his throat, but even as it did, he knew the voice did not belong to Lilith. Thomas turned, and a lovely girl in a blue surcoat with a white cotte beneath stood before him.

"I am Asneth," she curtsied. "Please follow me."

She brought him to a well-appointed bedchamber where a manservant waited with towels and a basin of warm water to help him wash the dirt of the road from his body.

"Are you Lord Zorac's kin, my lady?" Thomas asked courteously, as a male servant began to help him remove his heavy hauberk and chausses.

"No, my lord. My father sold me to a man who peddles flesh to men who wish to defile virgins. My lord Zorac bought me, untouched, and brought me here to educate me, teach me to run his household and care for his guests until I choose a husband of whom he approves. He says he may be someone I love," she considered him with a frank interest that was young and appealing, and Thomas could not help smiling.

"And are you supposed to allow his guests to take liberties with you?" he asked, shrugging out of the russet gambeson.

"Oh no, my lord." She raised her mischievous gaze to him. "My lord Zorac has warded my body. The man who attempts to handle me in an unchivalrous manner receives burned fingers." She placed her hand in the palm of his, as if to demonstrate, but he thought it might just be to test the fit of his palm and fingers around hers.

"Suitably biblical," Thomas murmured.

"Lilith services the guests in the manner in which you refer. She is my lord Zorac's Great Whore."

She flinched at his grip. He withdrew his touch.

"My pardon, lady. You startled me. Why is she made to do this?"

"She is being punished. My lord Zorac said her fate is divine justice to women who refuse to be satisfied by any man."

"Asneth," the manservant said. "Lord Zorac awaits his guest. We must prepare him."

"Of course," she curtsied to Thomas. "I leave you with John to help you bathe and change. I hope to see you again, Sir Thomas." She smiled at him, her innocence and hope for a suitor as fresh on her as dew on a leaf.

§

Thomas had a well-made hunter green tunic which he chose to wear over a natural linen shirt. He belted the tunic over tan hose that clung to his muscular thighs. Asneth returned, once he was attired, to brush out his hair and scrub the lingering grime of the road from beneath his nails and the crevices of his knuckles.

He was not a vain man, and normally he would have waved away such additional measures to make him more than adequately presentable. However, he wanted to look his best for his lady, no matter her state, and so he sat and allowed Asneth to comb out his hair. It lay just past his shoulders and she claimed it picked up the same color and shine of the copper threads embroidered along the edge of his tunic. She compared his eyes to the amber in a lion's gaze and made him smile with her earnest flirting. After the harsh training of the past few weeks, her youth was like the touch of sunshine, balancing the dark intensity of what lay ahead of him. The manservant laced up his thigh high velvet boots, and then Thomas followed Asneth to Zorac's great hall.

It was a small gathering that awaited him there. Zorac sat alone at the head of a polished long table that was embellished in an unusual manner. As he drew closer, Thomas saw a trained trellis of interwoven rose branches bordered the table's edge. It was approaching summer, so there were buds of a soft pink color preparing to burst forth among the thorns.

"It is an enchanting spell, sir," Thomas touched one of the unopened flowers.

"Nothing but the magic of the Goddess and the sweat of my gardener," Zorac said. "The man sanded the edge of the table, to give the runners a rough edge for their roots." Asneth stood close to the wizard's shoulder and he reached up and took her hand, making her smile when he pressed it to his lips. Thomas watched, intrigued, as the girl stroked his hair with adoration and the wizard accepted her touch with affection.

"The idea was Asneth's," Zorac explained. "She easily sees ways to turn the world around her as beautiful as her soul. And," the wizard added dryly, "it is a pretty way to inspire good manners. If you do not respect their beauty enough to keep from slumping on the table, the thorns you respect. It is an interesting exercise, to see which lesson my guests require to maintain their posture at dinner. But I have spoiled the test for you."

"I suspect there are other, more serious, tests you have in store for me," Thomas said.

Zorac chuckled and beckoned a servant forward to offer his guest wine. "Go from here, Asneth, and take supper with the servant women."

She curtsied, smiled again at Thomas, and took her leave.

At another table, several of the guardsmen ate their meal and spoke quietly amongst themselves, though now and then they cast an interested eye upon Thomas. The stable lad was there, and an older man, perhaps the gardener Zorac spoke about. The knight and the wizard were alone at the large table.

"You do not keep a large company here, my lord."

"I share my home with those humans whose company I can tolerate. That number is few."

"Your reputation beyond your borders is far more sinister than within them, sir," Thomas observed, taking a seat to Zorac's right at his gesture of invitation. "Your people seem well content with your rule."

"You and I both know that a man with powers that seem beyond a normal man's grasp is often feared, Sir Thomas."

Thomas held the wizard's keen gaze. "I know that often there is reason to fear a man with such power, for a man is still a man."

"Perhaps. How came you to be so serious of eye, Sir Thomas, with so few years upon you? You are not thirty, I'll wager. And yet I have heard of some of your courageous exploits."

"I was charged with the duties of a knight at a young age," Thomas replied.

"There is a legend," Zorac considered him with that same penetrating gaze, "that Arthur knighted a child, a mere peasant lad, before he went into the battle of Camlann."

"I have heard that legend as well, my lord."

"It was long ago, of course. Centuries. The legends say that this last knighting was special. The boy was blessed by that deed, and he aged more slowly than most, in order that he could make sure the tale of Arthur was known and never forgotten, that he could live his life as an enduring example of Arthur's dream."

"All power comes from God, my lord."

"Mmm. If the story is true, I suspect that would be a lonely life."

"To spread the word of a dream can compensate for many things, my lord."

"Not as the years continue to pass and men grow deaf. Then there is just loneliness."

Thomas took a casual swallow of wine. "Indeed, my lord. Do you find yourself lonely in the path you have chosen, that you would dwell on the loneliness of a legend?"

The wizard's power was a wash of heat, even without a flash of annoyance spiking it. Thomas held his posture, the wine to his lips, even as the table beyond them stilled, the men sensing the irritation of their master.

Zorac's gaze shifted from Thomas. "Enough of word games," he said abruptly. "Lady Lilith. Do not stand at the door like a shy maiden, for you are far from that. Come in and meet your guest."

Thomas's breath caught in his throat. He placed the goblet back on the table and turned, straddling the bench, so his face was averted from Zorac's scrutiny.

She was his dream. He knew she was more than his imagination, but to see her in the flesh, confirmation that his visions had been true, knocked his senses down, and rolled over them. The soul and body he craved were here before him now, within a few strides. He felt as if the air for his lungs would from this moment on be dependent on her very presence.

He smelled that sweet scent to the air, the scent from the dream, but in this reality, there was more to it. It had a woman's sexual secrets beneath it, her secrets. The fist holding his heart squeezed mercilessly.

She had auburn hair, the browns and reds glinting in the torchlight as she moved across the room. It was piled on her head, rather than free on her shoulders in the way of unmarried women. He wondered the weight of it did not bow that slender pale nape. She was one of those women with such fair skin that a faint freckling sprinkled her throat and the curve of her shoulders he could see. Rather than marring her, it added to the tapestry of her beauty.

She was small to have dominated so much of his dreams. All delicate bones, her wrists like works of porcelain. Her breasts were firm apples pressing against her bodice. Even the soft glide of her slippered feet on the fresh rushes aroused his senses.

The dress she wore was like nothing he had seen before. Her gown was black lace over an undergarment of sheer white fabric that showed the pale color of her skin through it. Her nipples were clearly visible to him, the deep blush aureoles drawing the eye as much as the prominent points sculpted by the fabric.

The black lace molded her bosom and waist, but was cut in ribbons at the skirt so it fluttered away from her as she walked. She wore no hose or undergarments, and so her dress exposed the body beneath, giving it only the modesty afforded by shadows of the hall's torchlight. With each step, he saw a length of thigh and calf, and the gates of paradise, the burnished curls over the opening of her tight cunt. For he knew from his dreams she would be the tightest of gloves, into which he would eagerly ease his fingers to test its warmth and fit. She had wide, generous hips that swayed as she moved, the pendulum swing enhanced by the fact her upper body seemed curiously immobile. Her walk was an undulation of sensual movement, as if she felt the stroke of a man's stiff cock with every step.

"No man can look at her and not want to bugger her arse," Zorac said flatly.

Thomas's gaze snapped to him, the crudity out of character with the demeanor of his host. The comment produced a coarse bark of laughter from the table of guardsmen. From their openly appreciative glances at Lilith, it was obvious they had been given that privilege often.

Thomas fought for calm, and watched as his lady's lips curved in the practiced suggestiveness of a whore, mocking their response. He knew as if it was his own reaction that she raised this shield against them, a challenging taunt to the wizard that held her captive. Thomas wondered if he were the only one who could see the cold and desperate quality to it, like the wounded soldier who thrust up from the ground for one more engagement, even as his life's strength waned from him.

He wanted her out of here. Away from them. Now. He forced himself to sit still, and impassive, and simply watch her, but he could not remember any challenge that had been harder for him.

"Come to me, first," Zorac commanded.

She passed the table of guardsmen. One reached out, stroked her breast, another her thigh, a quick fingering of her cunt through the clothes. She stopped at that touch, her facial features tightening in rigid reaction, and a soft gasp escaped her. The man chuckled, pushed her on her way with a sharp slap to her arse.

As difficult as it was for him to do so, Thomas turned his gaze from her to study his adversary. Zorac's face had gone flat and hard, not as if he saw a beautiful woman moving toward him, but something he detested with all his being, its very presence to be loathed.

As for Lilith, as she drew closer, Thomas saw her lips and jaw were taut and her dark eyes glassy, as if polished by a daily wash of tears. The skin stretched thin over her prominent cheekbones was like white stone polished to a soft satin luster by the constant flow of a waterfall.

Thomas noticed her fingers twitched in agitation at her sides. She wet her lips, and her eyes darted to Thomas and away, at least a dozen times as she crossed the hall. Her throat worked in nervous swallows. By the time she reached Zorac's side, her breath was coming in shallow pants.

"Ah, you like that we have a guest tonight, don't you, my lady Lilith?"

She shook her head, and Zorac chuckled, but Thomas saw nothing he would have called humor in the man's expression. "Sir Thomas, this is the Lady Lilith, who is, in fact, very pleased by your presence among us tonight. Let me show you."

The wizard reached out and drew back the lace cover. The threads of the sheer underdress that had rubbed between her thighs as she walked now shimmered with her honey.

Lilith made a soft noise of protest, frantic eyes shifting to Thomas's face.

"My lord, she is in pain," Thomas said.

"If she was, she would deserve it, but she is not, good sir, you may believe me, or believe the evidence of your nostrils. She is *in pleasure.*"

"But her arms," Thomas gestured. Lilith's arms had not risen from her sides during her walk across the room, nor now, when Zorac held her dress up, exposing her honeyed thatch to the view of Sir Thomas and the other interested men.

"They are capable of movement, at my command," Zorac explained. "Lilith does nothing except at my command. Is that not right, my little whore?"

Lilith's lips drew back from teeth wet with saliva. "Yes, my lord." Her voice was like air glinting with the soft gold of early morning. Her gaze was full of hate and lust at once.

"My lord," Thomas sat back, though his hands itched to do creative forms of violence. "You are making me very uncomfortable with your unkind treatment of this woman. I believe in courtly behavior toward women of all classes."

"Women like this make victims out of men like you," Zorac said, his eyes suddenly dangerous fire. Lilith made an abrupt noise of protest.

"It gets worse when I'm angered, doesn't it?" Zorac murmured. He took his hands away from her. She continued to stand beside him, shivering, but the wizard shifted his gaze to Thomas, ignoring her.

"There is a whimsical spell, Sir Thomas. It involves the resilient thread of the spider's web, which can hold its prey immobile until the spider decides to feed its hunger. And a strand of the lady's hair in question." His palm pressed the side of Lilith's fair cheek, his fingers caressing. She made an inconsolable noise, like a bereft soul faced with the hopelessness of hell, and turned her face into the wizard's hand. She bit him with passion, sucking on his skin. Her cheeks were flushed and she made a desperate noise of protest when he withdrew his hand and wiped it distastefully on his napkin. She looked away from Thomas's intent regard, her eyes filled with shame and uncontrolled hunger.

"Then, regretfully," Zorac continued, as if he had been interrupted by a dog begging for scraps at his elbow, "the spider, too, must go into the spell. For a true and strong binding always requires blood. What comes from this potion is a fabric, transparent like that web, so you cannot see it. That means you do not obscure from view that which you bind. My lady Lilith wears this spell on her arms, from elbows to wrists, binding their movement to her sides in the way you see. You can remove her clothes without disturbing it," Zorac leaned forward. With a sharp jerk, he pulled the soft fabric of her dress, from where it rested on the points of her shoulders, down to her waist. "So you need not be denied in any way."

Her breasts would be perfect in his palms, like fresh oranges. Thomas could well imagine the firm flesh giving way beneath his touch, quivering as she gasped, a bit breathless from his gentle kneading, the brush of his thumbs over those incredibly plump nipples. He had seen grapes in Italy like them, a deep burgundy color, begging to be taken into the mouth for the juices to come forth and fill every sense, not just stroke the taste buds.

She stood there, helpless to do anything but be exposed to the appreciative glance of every man in the room, including himself.

Thomas was shamed that even in this moment he felt such desire for her. Aye, he was hard as the stone bench on which he sat. However, unlike the other men, he desired to plunge himself into the hot wetness of her soul, penetrate and fuck that, until it shuddered around him and surrendered.

"The spell has many advantages, as you can imagine," Zorac took a sip of wine, never glancing at those perfect breasts, "but some drawbacks. While she wears the binding, Lilith is dependent on my hand for food and water, lest she cares to drink and eat from the floor with the dogs.

"At first, she spurned my hand, until she was so hungry she did scrounge for scraps with the dogs. The depths of her pride surprised me. She relented when I decreed that, if she would act like a dog, then she'd be fucked like one. It is something you do not often see," the wizard's impassive gaze shifted to Lilith, whose expression revealed nothing but her hunger. "A woman desperate to fulfil two needs at once, gulping down food from the floor as fast as she can, choking out moans between bites because a man is hammering her cunt from behind."

Thomas rose, his face hard. Zorac remained motionless, watching him. Lilith's dark, hopeless eyes studied the knight.

"What crime has this woman committed, my lord, that you feel she deserves to be shamed in this fashion?" the knight asked.

"This is not the public square, my lord Thomas, where sentences must be read aloud. Suffice it to say she has committed a sin for which this punishment is not nearly severe enough."

"You are God, then, to judge her so?"

Zorac leaned forward, his pale blue eyes glittering like ice in the longest days of winter. His lips curled back in a snarl. "In all things concerning her, I am. Hell's justice is slow, Sir Thomas. At time, Lucifer needs a hand to carry out God's sentences. And since I am God in this place, I think we shall now find out more about what brings you to us."

Thomas turned quickly as a guard came forward and dropped his saddlebags before the wizard.

"You usually go through your guest's belongings, sir?" Thomas asked coldly.

"I protect my interests, Sir Thomas." The wizard opened the flap of the saddlebag and peered in at the contents, but did not remove them. After a moment, he replaced the flap and sat back, considering the knight. "So your challenge is for the Lady Lilith, as I suspected," he said.

"It is." Thomas gauged in his mind the position of the guards in the room, and what he might have to do to defend himself or his lady. "And I would have told you that honestly, in our conversation tonight. I bring no intention of subterfuge, my lord. I am here for Lilith. I do not intend to leave without her."

Lilith's attention darted between the two of them, confusion altering her tense features.

"I see. You have brought tools to perform the ritual of awakening," Zorac said thoughtfully. "The High Priestess Helene has given some thought to what might overturn my spell, without offending me." He chuckled, startling Thomas with his sudden affability. "It is clever, I give her that. However, Helene overlooked one thing." The wizard's lips pulled back into a smile that enhanced the cruelty Thomas had suspected there. "There is no way this worthless whore can survive the ritual of awakening. There is nothing in her soul to awaken. It will destroy her hollow mind and you will leave here with less than the hope with which you came. Knowing that, I can afford to be a gracious host, and offer you something for your trouble. Show him your wiles, Lilith. Take off the dress."

"I do not require—"

"Do not make it worse on her," Zorac said, his voice sharp. Lilith's breath caught in her throat and her body shuddered. Her head dropped back on her shoulders and her fingers closed into fists. "Let me proceed, Sir Thomas, unless you enjoy seeing her torment heightened."

The muscles in Thomas's jaw flexed and he gave a bare nod. It was obvious the task of taking off the dress would not be an easy one for a woman with her arms bound. Thomas supposed that was the point, to humiliate her further by making her do the crude maneuvers before them all.

With a steel glance at the wizard, he stepped upon the table, and down to stand before her. Now he was within touching distance, nothing between them but air. Despite his objection to their surroundings for their first face-to-face meeting, he felt as though his emotions would burst from him like his seed. She was so small, the top of her head just at his collarbone. Her breasts swayed with her uneven breaths.

"I will help you, my lady," he said.

She looked up at him, her eyes like the depths of a man's soul. Thomas was conscious of Zorac watching them, but the wizard made no protest, which was fortunate for him. This close to her, feeling her pain, smelling the scent of her arousal, Thomas would have cheerfully drawn his sword and gutted him for defiling what was his.

For she was his. He had known it in his dreams, but now, here, this close to her, it was as plain and miraculous a fact as the color of her hair. She was his, whatever her imperfections or mysteries. She was his heart. He could feel it beat faster in his breast as it recognized her.

He went to one knee and set his hands to her bare rib cage. Heat. Her skin was so warm to be so fair. At his touch, her lips parted and moistened, a flush spreading across her throat and fair shoulders. Thomas reached around her, bringing her a step closer to him inside the span of his arms, in order to ease the back lacing of the gown and take the full ensemble down over her hips. Her breasts were no more than a finger width from his face, and he saw the blue veins just below the milky skin.

The bare curves of her buttocks molded into his palms as he brought the fabric down over them. As he guided the dress to her ankles, his thumbs curved over her thighs and he touched wetness. He slid his fingers forward and found that there was a track of moisture trickling from her. He smelled her arousal like an exotic musk wafting from an infidel's tent, offering forbidden pleasures. The visible area of her cunt was a red full rose, slick with a dew that only the heat of a man's lips, like the sun, could absorb.

"You see, my lord," Zorac spoke. "I told you true. She is not in pain, but frozen in pleasure. She cannot go forward, or back. I have perfected the spell which keeps a woman on the cusp of that *petite morte*, never quite there, but not able to withdraw from its heights, so she is always off balance, teetering on the edge of a cliff from which she can neither leap nor retreat."

"Pleasure meets pain, and—"

"The two never separate. It is the reality which most of us choose not to face. Lilith bears the lesson every day. Let me show you how pleasure can bring agony." Zorac motioned to one of his guardsmen.

"I need no such demonstration," Thomas said, though he knew his words to be cursedly untrue. Helene had counseled him.

It will be difficult, my lord, to see her thus, but that is why I have taught you to discipline your most primitive of instincts, including aggression. Before you begin the ritual, you must be sure you understand fully the type of spell she is under.

He wished a dire curse on all priestesses and wizards, but called on the discipline of a lifetime to stay where he was and say no more. *Forgive me, my lady.*

Her eyes were glazed, and she was leaning forward awkwardly, without the balance of her arms, as if the throbbing between her legs were making it impossible for her to straighten. Thomas steadied her, closing his hands on her shoulders, and she pressed her forehead into his shoulder.

The guardsman Zorac had called over was a burly fellow of mature years, with a stern but not unkind air about him. A captain of the guard, perhaps. He stood behind Lilith and looked down into Thomas's dangerous expression.

He shifted his glance to Zorac, and the wizard nodded. "It is fine, Cullen. The knight will not interfere, not if he values his lady."

Cullen did not look as if he feared a fight. "My lord Zorac knows the ways to mete out justice and mercy, sir," the guardsman said, addressing Thomas. "His actions may seem harsh, but he has been just to me. I would not serve him otherwise."

Thomas did not speak, his expression reflecting his barely contained fury. Cullen shrugged, and his eyes went to the tempting bare arse offered before him. The combination of that and the wizard's encouragement overcame his concerns with Thomas. He pulled aside his woolen hose and braies, and thrust his erect and impressively-sized cock into Lilith from behind.

The jerk of her body against his hands was like a mortal blow to Thomas's chest. In his travels, he had been forced to witness things he wished he had not seen, participate in things he wished he could have avoided. Even before Helene's regimen, he had mastered the art of keeping his emotions chained down in order to learn from what he saw, and act to prevent even greater suffering when he could.

This should be no different, except it was his lady being dishonored while he stood and allowed it for the sake of her ultimate freedom. It was a bitter taste in his mouth, like the blood that spilled onto his tongue, from his teeth grinding into the meat of his cheek.

The man's hand spread over Lilith's bare back, her ridge of spine, and pushed her down further to make the entry smoother. Her forehead now pressed against Thomas's chest.

He held her as the man grunted and thrust. Her legs spread to accommodate him. She threw her head up, her teeth bared. She moaned, a long, lonely cry of passion that would stir the loins of any man.

Please—" she gasped. "Please—"

"No, my lady," Zorac said, devoid of mercy. "Feel Cullen's cock in your cunt, feel yourself hanging on that precipice, like a man on the gallows just a moment from the gates of Paradise. Know that the pleasure will just build and build, and there will be no release, just pleasure that becomes the greatest of agonies to bear."

"Hold,...my...me..." she managed, her eyes on Thomas, tearing.

Thomas collared her throat with one hand to keep her balanced, and caught the fingers of her left hand, bound to her side, in his own. Her grip was spasmodic, but the intimate link made her eyes close. The tears spilled free, marking her cheeks, even as her cries became more guttural, a woman trembling on the edge of climax.

She surged forward, her mouth devouring Thomas's, her tongue wet and sweet in his mouth.

"Sweet Blood of Christ, but she's always so tight," Cullen managed. His thighs slapped hard and loud against her arse, as if he rode the body of a galloping mare. He groaned, long and low, the sound of a man releasing his seed, his fingers clutching her hips in a bruising grip.

Lilith wailed, not in pleasure but in frustration. He finished and pulled out of her, as matter of fact as a man finished relieving himself against a tree. She would have jerked around, but Thomas held her as the man withdrew.

"No, no..." her other hand strained toward herself but of course could not reach. The man adjusted himself, did a half bow to Zorac, and resumed his place at the nearby table. Thomas noticed, despite his professed loyalty to the wizard, that Cullen did not meet anyone's eyes.

"No, no..." her lips and teeth sought Thomas's face, neck and ears as she thrashed like an animal in a trap in his grasp. Her hair had come down, and with her teeth bared, she looked like a forest sprite on a rampage for a man's blood and virility both.

"She will calm down in a few moments," Zorac assured Thomas. "She has gotten very good at controlling herself. I used to spread her out on the floor and manacle her to keep her from doing harm to herself. Her scent perfumed our meal and reminded my men of the delights of the night to come. Of course, they had to take her there, on the flagstones, because the spell gets worse with every man who takes her. She can become quite dangerous, more wild than any wounded animal I have ever seen."

Thomas rose to his feet, holding Lilith against his side.

There was a scramble of activity, steel being pulled. The guardsmen were there, and Cullen stood at his lord's shoulder, his sword out. Thomas wondered if Zorac had called to them in their minds, or if his expression alone had warned them he was a breath away from taking their lord's head.

"Would you strike me down, Sir Thomas," Zorac said, his expression as dangerous as that of a falcon sighting a lone fox kit, "if you thought it would free her?"

Thomas did not blink. Every muscle of his body was tight with restrained power screaming to be unleashed.

"If I thought that was the answer to this," he said in measured tones, "to save my lady from a wretched fate such as you have designed for her, yes, I would. You would not rise from that chair again, no matter what men or magic you have to command."

The guards shifted, muttering, but Thomas's attention did not waver from the man before him. "But it is not the answer," he said, after a charged silence. "The answer lies in her heart, and yours. I cannot influence yours. Hers I can win."

"You are foolish, sir," Zorac scoffed at him. "I am not isolated here. I know the few knights who still pursue quests of honor whisper of her, and wonder if they should embrace the challenge of defeating an evil wizard such as myself to win one of the most beautiful women in our world, though she is only of basic noble birth. But in the end, they realize there is no real glory or wealth in it, just some fleeting notoriety and a well-used whore. So they think of it, but do not come.

"You have come," he cocked his golden head, "and with the endorsement of the mysterious Lady Helene. However, I wonder if, by morning, you will decide Lilith is a prize not worth winning and simply ride away. I have patience, and am willing to wait and see."

"Then, sir, I would prefer to take the lady to bed now," Thomas said. "I demand the spell be removed from her wrists. It gives me no advantage with the ritual, and you know it."

"I know that, but the binding stays, Sir Thomas. Do not presume on my hospitality any further than you have. Your challenge intrigues me, that is all. At this moment, you, and your arrogance, endure on my sufferance."

The two men locked gazes for several more tense moments, and then Thomas inclined his head. "My lord."

It was as much permission as he would seek. He lifted Lilith in his arms. She was far too light, and it further infuriated him that Zorac had not nourished her as he should. He stepped around the table, his contemptuous gaze raking the guardsmen before he exited the room. Lilith's damp cheek pressed against his heart.

Chapter Three

His chambers had been attended while he was gone. The servants had left a tub of water by the fire for morning washing, and some bread and cheese on a board for late evening appetites. The bed was made up with a heavy mound of covers.

Lilith had begun struggling in his arms halfway up the stairs, attempting to rub herself against him, making little mewling cries. Thomas set her on her feet in the chamber, holding her away from him. She fought him, but he was much stronger, and simply waited until she raised angry, agonized eyes to his.

"No," he said softly. "You cannot do anything for yourself that way, lady. You know that. Be calm and strong, as you have taught yourself to be. Be calm."

He kept his hands still, so as not to add to her agitation, though he ached to stroke her hair away from her face, touch those lips, give her the comfort and protection of his body.

Her eyes squeezed shut as he held her. In a few moments, her writhing became a rhythmic rock against his grip, like a metronome settling to a slower pace. At length, she stopped moving and opened her eyes, gazing at him.

"It feels like almost dying or almost being born," she said, surprising him with her sudden coherence. "Not quite finished, trapped between world and dust, or womb and world. I am afraid one day I will be torn in two and yet still live." Her attention roamed from his eyes, and she looked at his hair, his forehead, the slope of his shoulder. "I dreamed of you," she said. "You disappeared in the mist."

"I will not do so again, milady," Thomas said, his throat tight at her lost eyes and trembling, roused body. "Come lie down for me, on the bed."

She stared at him, as if she might refuse, but then she shrugged and turned, bringing a peculiar grace to the action, since she had to move slowly to balance herself without the use of her hands. The bend of her knee to take the mattress and the turn of her hips showed him the deep pink folds of her damp cunt, the sway of her breasts, the nipples tight from cool hallways and bespelled arousal.

"Lie back and open your legs to me," he said.

She tossed her head, another tendril of red hair sliding free of its bindings. Her hair was more than half undone by the rough fucking she had received and her own struggles. As she turned on her hip, and began to lay back, he moved forward. He caught her head in the palms of both of his hands, arresting her body in mid-recline. She trembled, her torso parallel with the diagonal tilt of his own, less than a handspan between the meeting of their hips, stomachs, chests, and lips. Thomas cradled the back of her skull in one hand and freed her hair.

Ribbons came loose, and he flicked pins away so fire spread over his fingers. He eased her back and his palms came forward, tumbling her thick mane over her shoulders and covering her breasts. She was freshly fallen snow before his gaze, with a swirl of fire at her center, like the color of her hair.

"Open your legs, Lilith," he repeated. "Show yourself to me."

"You are not my Master. I am not yours to command," she said, but her voice was weak.

"I am your Master. You know it, or you would not try to refuse me. You would be as you are to all the others, indifferent to them, while your body is desperately compliant. You are my lady."

His hands were on her thighs, and he eased them open. They shivered, like the lean bodies of two soft white rabbits, unmoving under human touch but remarkably feral in their shuddering response, so there was no doubt that he touched something wild and untamed. How often had he seen kings and lords keep ferocious animals in chains or cages in their halls? They wanted that exotic beauty within touching distance, they wanted the animal's wildness. They put the animal in a cage, making him dependent on scraps. He went mad or listless, only a shadow of the wild creature he once was. The captor sucked away the animal's wildness, and became the beast instead.

His wild creature was spread for him now, her whole body shuddering in a way that made him want to cover her, surround her, feel her fragile thighs and breasts against him. He wanted to warm them with his heat and protection, fill her tight channel with his cock, lock them together as one being.

There was a glitter at her nipples he had not noticed in the hall. He bent and looked closer. "What are these?" he asked. He grazed his fingers over the slim silver circlet around her full left nipple.

She writhed at his touch, but managed an answer. "They make them more aroused, larger. It pleases my lord for me to wear them."

"Lilith," Thomas sat on the edge of the bed. He bent, his breath hovering over one engorged nipple. "You will not call Zorac 'my lord' any longer. He is not your Master. I am."

Her brow furrowed, and she began to shake her head in denial. He laid his lips over the tip of the right nipple and pulled it and much of the breast around it into his mouth. Lilith arched off the bed, crying out, her fingers straightening at her sides, as if extending all the digits would make up for her helpless vulnerability to all he could do to her.

His act had a very functional purpose, though suckling her sweet tits and feeling her moan beneath his touch swelled his cock to a painful thickness that made him lightheaded. His rage, lust and desire had all fueled the erection. He wanted to use it as a weapon, and he fully intended to do so.

There was not much difference between him and Zorac in that regard. Helene was right. Thomas wanted to free

Lilith from Zorac, but not make her free. She was his. However, he wanted to claim her rightfully.

She would fight him, he knew, for he had to prove himself worthy of being her Master. Thomas's lips curved into an unexpected smile on the fleshy curve of her breast. Goosebumps rose under his lips as the cool air mixed with the heated flow of his breath. It was as Arthur had been known to say. Might is not right; might should be used *for* right.

This was right.

He had both tiny circlets in his mouth, slick with his saliva, and he spat them out onto the floor. "You will not need such things to stay roused for me, my lady," he said. "You will experience full pleasure tonight at my command, I promise you."

If he did the cursed ritual right. Fighting a border war was far easier than this.

Thomas rose, moved down the bed and spread her legs wider. He attached them to the cuffs Zorac had left at the corner posts, apparently to contain Lilith for his guests' pleasure. He did not wish to use them, but knew he must. They were tools and he must not give them any more significance than that. Thomas shut out the misery of their immediate surroundings, the ways Zorac had tortured her, his fury with the wizard. He had found her, they were together, he must make this work. It was that simple. The room was a room anywhere, with the comforts any man who had served in battle could appreciate.

"My Lord Thomas," she murmured, and the words nearly brought him to his knees.

"My lady."

"I do not know if I can bear more pleasure. It is something about you that...opens me, inside. I am afraid I cannot bear it."

"It will be all right, Lilith. Do not fear."

He turned, a basin and a wet cloth now in his hand, and studied her in the flickering light. Her body twitched, little ripples of movement, a press of hips into the bed, a thrust of breasts upward, a restless toss of her head, all movements of a woman wanting a man upon her, inside her, movements she could not control. Artificial cravings Zorac had instilled in her.

He came to her, and her gaze centered on the empty basin in his hand.

"I want you to relieve yourself in this, my lady," Thomas said, sliding his hand under her back and lifting her so she was upon it.

Her cheeks stained with color. "My lord, I am noble born, and will not—"

"Be still, and obey me, lady. There is no shame here. I will not have you suffer the smell of another man's seed forced upon your lovely cunt. Relieve yourself and I will wash you. His eyes burned down into hers. "No man, other then me, will ever have you again."

She swallowed, her lips tight. She closed her eyes, averted her face, and a moment later he heard the trickle in the basin as she purged herself of Cullen's issue.

He set the basin aside and set to work on her with the cloth. Her thighs tensed at his gentle ministrations, and her back arched at the pleasure of his touch.

"It is such a small thing," he said, dropping to one knee. He was tall, so she could still see him. "You see?"

She gasped, as he laid his thumb on that bud of sensitive flesh just above her warm and moist opening. It was the barest of touches, but it stayed there, a light, immobile pressure that transformed her small movements into hard spasms.

"A tiny thing, smaller than my thumb pad, but it is so much of what you are, Lilith. It has such power, for you, from you. It is the center, your power and your vulnerability at once. But it is not your heart. Only your heart can tell you what Master's hand you will choose to welcome within." He exerted a small pressure and she cried out, her fingers clutching the folds of blankets beneath her.

"You must give me your heart with your sweet cunt," he slid his thumb down, and teased the slippery folds as she writhed, her teeth clenched against his emotional and physical assault. "Call me Master and renounce Zorac's hold on you."

"I am under his spell," she managed. "I can do nothing."

"You can do everything, you simply must choose," he said.

He left her to think on that, disposed of the contents of the basin. He took the amulet he wore from his neck, left it by the fire, and then brought another basin, this one filled with clean warm water.

Lilith looked up at him, her lips parted. He indulged himself, leaning down to cover that mouth with his own. She murmured against him, incoherent, urgent noises. He cupped his hand behind her neck, holding her firmly, feeling the stroke and dart of her tongue against his own, painting her with the wetness of his mouth, letting her get to know him as he was getting to know her. He pulled back. He could not smile at her protesting whimper, as he would have if she was truly free to make the choice to be bound to him. There was too much animal desperation in her face, a feral need that was beyond the pleasures of sexual teasing.

Zorac had lied. He had not introduced her to a marriage of pleasure and pain, but the mutation of pleasure into pain, a pain she embraced because of her body's unnaturally heightened response. It filled Thomas with hard anger anew. She could do harm to herself in this state, allow a man to fuck her with the dagger he used to cut his meat as readily as his cock. He wondered at the "pleasures" Zorac's guests might have tested against the spell.

Would she be able to survive what had been done to her, even if he broke the spell? Maybe, if she made the choice, and let Thomas be the Master who stood by her side to help her heal.

He had to put such thoughts aside for now. You must pretend you are a surgeon in the battle field, Helene had said. You must amputate and bleed the patient without letting your emotions interfere. He wondered how a surgeon would feel if the one coming under the knife was his lady, his heart and soul.

Thomas settled down beside her thigh and stroked the curve of her waist. "You are beautiful in every way, Lilith," he said, his voice a rumble against the muted pop and crackle of the fire.

She swallowed, fighting visibly for some control over the roar of her body. God knew she must have enough practice doing so.

"I am not, my lord. My beauty is only in my skin. My heart and soul are far too black for the purity of yours."

Thomas glanced sharply at her. Up until now, her voice had held frustration and not a little anger. This was resigned despair. She believed her words.

"Zorac is an evil man who enjoys having a woman with your beauty under his thrall."

"You do not believe that."

Thomas lifted a brow. "He has done you harm, Lilith. For that alone, I would take his life."

"You have seen Elias, the stable boy. Cullen, Asneth. They are here as the acts of a man who desires to save and preserve innocence that has been lost, and protect the wounded. Why would Zorac punish me, if there was not a blackness in my soul deserving of punishment? You would do better to leave here and—"

He laid his fingers on her lips. They parted beneath his touch and he stroked them, one at a time. Her tongue came out and kissed his skin, just a slight curl of the wet tip against the sensitive skin between his knuckles.

Thomas turned from her, and brought the amulet he had left by the fire. The disk was now heated by the flame.

"This is a coin I found at Camlann. It is from Arthur's time, from that battle."

Lilith's face revealed the effort it took her to focus on his words.

"You were lucky to find it, my lord. So much has been looted from that place, or carried away as relics."

"Indeed." He held it up to the light, a simple dented piece of silver strung on a much more expensive chain of beaten silver. A cross was still faintly visible in the center of the coin. "I look at it and think it perhaps fell out of some man's pouch or pocket while he fought. Perhaps he would have used the money for an ale, or to buy a lady a trinket. I kept it, to remind myself how close death and life are to one another, and how the quiet of peace is only a breath away from the rage of battle. Love and hate are the two sides to this coin. Light and dark are in us all, Lady Lilith, and they are both necessary to make us complete."

He stroked the heated metal over the blood-filled petals of her sex, eliciting a soft cry from his lady's throat. He dipped the amulet in the basin of water and lifted it, allowing the water from it to drip into his palm.

Thomas moved his wet hand over her hips, turning his fingers downward. A single drop slid from his palm to hang on the tip of his middle finger, centered so she stared down the length of her body at it as it hovered there, clinging to his skin. It grew fatter, as more water from his palm trickled down and joined it.

"This shall fall right on that tiny spot above your weeping cunt, my lady," Thomas said. "It shall feel like the press of a lover's tongue there. Watch it glisten, think of its impact as it—" the drop loosed from his finger, "...falls."

Lilith's thighs strained up against the manacles holding her legs open as the drop plunked against her, where he said it would.

"You will not argue with me, lady," Thomas said, continuing to hold his hand above her. Another drop gathered at the tip of his finger, gained size, sparkled in the firelight. "Or hide your thoughts from me. Will you?"

"No, my lord," she gasped as another fell, then another. Her hips thrust upward.

"Good. You must trust me, Lilith. Why does Zorac punish you?"

"I cannot..." Lilith's words caught in her throat as another drop hit. Thomas watched it melt on her hot folds. He watched the way the curve of her arse cheeks, visible between her open legs, flattened as she pushed her hips down into the pallet. He shifted, straddling her spread thighs with his own muscular ones, settling so he held her thighs down, immobilizing her hips. He dipped his amulet, let another drop fall. She made a strangled cry.

"My lord, you cannot...please do not torture me so,...I cannot..."

He cupped the water now in the shallow basin of his palm, and the drops falling off his fingers became a rapid tattoo of rainfall on her. Lilith moaned, her breasts swelling impossibly rounder before his eyes, the nipples turgid points. Her thighs were tight beneath his own as he kept her still, forcing all sensation to come from that one still point of her body. He was aware of the arched column of her throat, her gasping breaths, her pleas, the clench of her hands at her sides. Yet his eyes never left that small area of flesh, and he hit it every time, his aim unerring.

"Fire is first, because fire is, of all the elements, the most transitory," he murmured. "The sun may or may not shine down upon you from one day to the next, but you anticipate, you shiver, and the sun comes forth.

"Fire heats water, but water touches fire, and fire is vanquished. Fire and water, the east coming to vanquish the south, a circle turning backwards, ending what has been done. We will travel from the most mutable elements to the most immutable, and when you are one with that most immutable fifth element, which is the Spirit, you will decide for yourself whether to accept and choose."

He had thought when he began the ritual, the words he had been taught would be stilted on his tongue, but he looked upon his lady and felt the heat she generated, the sweat of her thighs trapped beneath him. The words came as natural to him as a battle cry.

"Let your waters vanquish the fire, lady," he urged, his voice a husky caress, affected by his own arousal. He felt no shame for it now. He would create a sacred place for the two of them in this wretched castle, and there would be no sin of lust. Lust was only a sin if it was a physical response with no spiritual basis, like eating too much meat or sweets and then having the desire to vomit, to cleanse oneself of the taint of excess. He could never have an excess of Lilith.

The priestess's words were in his mind, her wise, beautiful eyes. His lips moved, repeating the invocation to fire and water again. The air grew even warmer around them. Lilith's gaze rested on his cock, straining hard and prominent against his hose, over her eager opening.

"Not time for that yet," he said. "Not until you choose, lady. Then, if you choose rightly, I will bring you so many pleasures. I will bring you a comb for your hair. I will feed you tender meats from my own fingers. I will give you a hard ride on an early morning when you first wake. My stiff cock will penetrate your tight, slippery channel and remind you each day which Master you embrace."

"I have no such choice to make, my lord. Zorac—"

He was perspiring, and a drop from his forehead fell. The sweat of his brow struck at the same moment as the water from amulet to palm. Lilith's back bowed up against her restraints, and her face showed her shock.

Thomas watched, suspended in an agony of male arousal, his dripping fingers over her sex as the flesh quivered, rippled and then spasmed, a flush rushing outward across her hips and pale belly. As the drips slowed from one palm, he poured a full trickle of water upon her from the other, keeping the tattoo of sensation unrelenting, dragging her release from her body with grim force of will and the overwhelming power of water itself.

Lilith screamed, her fingers digging into her thighs, her heels thrusting into the bed. She strained hard beneath him, a rhythmic, primitive dance. The tidal wave came, and she was on it, riding it so powerfully that she choked on her own saliva and began to cough, her distress no deterrent to the strangled groans that the climax ripped from her throat.

"Sshh, sshh, easy, lady," Thomas leaned forward, as the first wave passed. He set the amulet aside, careful not to touch her soaked cunt with any part of his body. It was still contracting with the aftershocks of her hard orgasm. He soothed her brow with one hand, letting her suck on the fingertips of the other one by one, not like an aroused woman, but a nursing child seeking comfort. She suckled fervently.

"It will not last long, my lady," Thomas told her, stroking her working jawline. "Zorac's spell still holds sway over you, and the desire will come back quickly, but be comforted in the knowledge I will bring you pleasure at least one more time this night."

"How did you,...what did you..."

"It is not easy to explain, my lady, but I will bring forth your pleasure, using each of the four elements. It circumvents Zorac's spell, for he only thought to think of a man sating his lust for you with his body. Cock, hands or mouth. Though he had enough forethought to make sure he prevented you from taking your pleasure with your own hands."

She flushed.

"You must not have any shame with me," he admonished her with a stern look, and indulged his own pleasure, covering her still pulsing sex with his hand to let her know his touch, before Zorac's spell returned to her in full force. She was silk and velvet both, and he was hard pressed not to dip into her heat. He felt the folds of skin shiver beneath his fingers. "I will, once we are free of here, command you to make yourself come with your own touch while I watch. It is a true pleasure most men have not discovered, nor most women. Zorac's spell prevents such an act from doing anything now but inflaming you.

"The elements, however, are not from men. Once all four elements have served you, the circle will be closed around you, and there is a final test, one that neither Zorac nor I can fight. You must open that place you are so unwilling to open, let me in and accept me for what I truly am to you. You will be stubborn," he smiled at her confused face, "because you are, and because you are frightened. But I am here, Lilith. I will not leave you."

"It comes again, my lord," she said, and the desolation in her voice pained him. He knew, despite his words, she had hoped the moment of respite had heralded the end to her torture. He forced his voice to remain even.

"So it does. I must lift you out of the bed now and take off this damp coverlet, before it wets the covers beneath you."

He unfastened the manacles at her ankles and lifted her body in his arms. His erection pressed against her hip and he nearly groaned at the pleasure of the soft flesh against the hard.

"You may take me, my lord," she said quietly. "Ease your frustration."

It cost her much to say it, he was sure. He could feel Zorac's hold stealing back over her body, parting her lips, transforming her features with that hunger.

This woman is mine, he raged, the anger surging up in him, tightening his grip. It was the aggression of a dominant, responding to the infringement of another into his rightful territory.

It came to him then, that a sexual purge to his own tension would aid them both. It would steady his focus, release some of his anger. And it would give him an additional opportunity to undermine Zorac's hold on her. Not by magic, not by machinations of wizards or priestesses, but by an act of will. He removed the cover, set her on her feet and pressed her to her knees on the floor. He took a seat in the carved chair in front of her, by the fire.

"Zorac has made you into a dog in heat, seeking your own pleasure." At her pained flush, he reached forward, cupped her face in a gentle hand. "But you have a will that stands separate from any magic I do or he does.

"I want you to accept my seed into your mouth, my lady, to give me pleasure, seeking none for yourself."

"I have not done this for any man," she said, her tone resentful, suspicious.

"It pleases me to see your spirit, lady. It is not an act of humiliation," he said. "You offer me a gift, as great an act of fealty as that of a knight who kneels to his liege lord. That fealty is a promise to serve the lord, as long as he lives by the principles in which the knight believes, and treats the knight honorably. Will you offer me that, my lady?"

"This ritual you are undertaking to free me, it will not work unless I do this?"

"It may work without it. This is a step, but not one that is required."

Her brow lowered, her eyes on the space between his booted feet.

"What do you prefer, lady, mutton or fowl?"

Her gaze snapped back to him. "Pardon, my lord?"

Thomas smiled, shook his head. "What does it feel like, his spell?" he asked, to distract her from the decision she faced. "Tell me true, lady. There need be no formality between us."

She hesitated, her glance shifting to the fire. "I will tell you, my lord, but you must do something to help me."

"Anything, my lady."

"Please put your hand over my eyes so I do not have to see you when I say the words."

He nodded, and cupped his hands over her eyes, pressing his callused palm against the soft skin of her cheeks and forehead, the brush of her lashes.

"It is as if a man's lance is always there, stroking," she said, in an embarrassed whisper. "I feel it there and in my other opening,...my arse, at the same time. There are mouths on my nipples, biting and sucking every moment. Hands stroke my hips, my stomach, my neck, and yet there is no one, as if this wall of pleasure separates me from all else. To walk, to eat, requires so much concentration. I sleep little, and when I do, my dreams are decadent, horrible pleasures."

Her mouth tightened, and Thomas brushed the side of his smallest finger over her top lip. "He sends me perverse dreams. I am with animals, with women, with two men at once who care naught for me, who hurt me, and I do not care..." her voice faltered. "Even...with children."

Thomas laid his other hand on her twitching shoulder and her head bowed, pressing into his palm. "Then you came into my dream. I knew it did not come from him, and for a time I could bear the other dreams, knowing you might be there, somewhere."

He took his hand from her face, leaned forward and gripped her hand down at her hip. Her palm sweated with her growing need. "You gave me some peace," she said, looking up at him, so close to her. "Though in my dream of you, I always became a monster at the end. Was it not so in your dream?"

"You succumbed to the spell at the end," he said. "But it was a dream, lady. Just a dream."

Her face crumpled. "Perhaps I am where I should be, my lord. You must at least consider that."

"You are a young woman, Lilith," Thomas said. "Barely out of childhood. How much evil can you have spread in the world?"

"Once, a young man betrayed his friend for silver..." her

voice trembled. "One unforgivable act."

"And yet he was forgiven," Thomas reminded her.

She laid her head down against him and he fondled her hair, his hand under it at her neck, soothing, though he regretted his touch would also incite her to a greater degree of arousal.

"You know, we met once, my lady," he said. "When I came back from a campaign, and delivered a message to your uncle's home." He looked down and saw she was listening, her eyes on the fire, perspiration beading on her top lip. "I passed you on the gallery. You wrinkled your nose, pointed, and said to your friends that knights who stunk like the pigs should stay in the stable area."

"And what did you do?" she managed, her cheek soft against his hand, her bosom lifting and falling quickly against his calf.

"I kept walking, and smiled at a spoiled child's ignorance. I thought how pretty she was, and how lovely a woman she would make, when time and experience had softened her edges."

"There is nothing soft about me now."

"I beg to differ, lady. You have many soft spaces, but you are strong. I cannot begin to imagine how you have kept from madness through five years of such torment."

She shook her head against his muscled thigh. "It was just survival, my lord. A coward's fear of death more than hell's torment. If I can bear this moment, I can survive the next moment, then the next, and then the day is done. That is all. Sometime, I just, became...apart."

"Like you were there, but not?"

She nodded, looking up at him with the question in her eyes.

"On the battlefield," he explained, "the horror and death, like men, stack up around you. Taking it moment by moment, not thinking back or forward from it, is one way to survive. As you hack into the flesh of another man and he screams and dies at your feet, you become something separate from yourself, in order that you can go to the next man and do the same thing."

He heard his voice become dispassionate, but knew the

shadows of the horrors lay in his amber eyes for her to see. "You are much stronger than you realize, Lady Lilith."

She gazed at him for a long moment. "This thing you ask me to do, with my mouth. It will bring you pleasure, my lord?"

"It will, all the more because it will bring it to you."

She turned, bracing her shoulder on the inside of his thigh so she could be square in between his spread legs. "Then, my lord," she said, "let me attend to you."

Thomas nodded. He drew his tunic up so the curve of his groin in the snug hose was revealed. He pushed the cloth aside, along with the folds of his braies beneath.

His cock came free, hard and attentive, and her eyes widened.

"I have...I have never done this, my lord."

"Put your mouth on it, as far down as you can reach, and then you slide your lips and tongue up and down. If your hand was free," he took his own and wrapped his grip at the base, stifling a deep grunt at the sensation, "it would be here, and move the same way."

"And I...stay on my knees."

"Yes," he looked down at her, her uncertain mouth only a breath away from his aroused organ. "When I come, you will swallow my seed, taking it within your belly." He passed a thumb along her cheek, a caress and a sensual command. "Do not spill a drop."

Lilith looked at his engorged lance. Slowly, so slowly he thought he might die, she leaned forward, her arse hovering above her heels, and she took him into the hot cavern of her mouth.

He had not been paying her false flattery. He knew what suffering was, and had some understanding of what could happen to the mind and soul of a person forced to endure torment each day, year after year. She had a courage and strength that he had rarely encountered, in man or woman. And she was not even aware of it.

He touched her bare shoulder, gripped it in his fingers. He felt the fragile network of bones, traced the light scattering of pale freckles across paler skin. Watched her head move gracefully up and down, her lovely mouth stretched around the length of him, felt the slide of her tongue along the pulsing vein that ran along the bottom length of his shaft. He could have come in her mouth in an instant, but the priestesses had taught him better. He must give her time to experience the pleasure of servicing him, learn his taste, crave the challenge of drawing his seed forth to her and only her.

She began to suck as well as stroke and he let out a deep, uneven breath. His lady learned quickly and he shuddered as he heard her make a soft noise in the back of her throat, a tentative purr of pleasure to answer his gasp. Her dark eyes flicked up to look at him and he caressed her chin with his hand, light touches that did not interfere with her movement, but which kept her gaze on his face so she could see his joy in her, his absorption with only her.

He shifted his hips forward to rock in rhythm with her movements, pushing himself deeper into her mouth, a little harder, demanding more of her. She made a surprised noise, gagged a bit and then adjusted. He smelled her scent and knew the friction of her cunt moving against her calves was adding to her arousal, but he thought there might be more than frustrated desire from Zorac's curse coursing through her veins. Her expression reflected the change in his, the growing tension in his features.

His touch on her shoulder became a convulsive clutch that moved up to her neck, then he gave up on a caress entirely and his fist tightened ruthlessly in her hair. She made a growling sound deep in her throat, a challenge and invitation. Some of his milky substance slid out from beneath her lips and started down his shaft. It escaped only a moment before she slid back down, using it to oil him further.

Thomas could tell she was feeling it, something she had not had for so long, like the first touch of precious sugar on a child's tongue. Control. Self-direction. A sense of self. A sense of choice. What started out in her mind as serving his pleasure, had brought him under her dominion. When pleasure became excruciating like this, the dominant became the slave of the servant. At this moment he was more certain than ever that he would do anything for her.

"Soon, my lady, when the spell is broken," he managed in a ragged voice, "you will do this to prepare me, and I will thrust in you, a hard sword impaling you, and fill you with pleasure."

She moaned, and he pushed her speed with his hand tangled in her hair, taxing her strength and the limits of her delicate jaw. He watched the soft flesh of her throat work as he strove to penetrate her as deeply as he could.

"Be ready, my lady," he rasped. He held her firm and his cock contracted. The room got hazy, narrowing to just her and that glorious mouth sucking on him, stroking furiously as he exploded, jetting hot streams of seed into the back of her throat, demanding she take him, accept him.

He held nothing back. He let her see the snarl of feral pleasure on his lips, in his eyes, hear the deep male groan of release, see his buttocks tighten up like drawn bows against the seat of the chair, his skin glowing with sweat from his movements in and out of her mouth.

She was choking, but holding her own. His seed came from the corners of her mouth, but she quickly swallowed and dove down another blessed stroke on painfully sensitive skin to collect every drop. It made desire sharpen in his belly again to see his lady attend him so well. He shoved down the sudden fear that he might fail in his task and not win her from this place.

When at last he was done, his grip did not immediately ease. "You are my lady," he said it out loud, giving power to the words, as if stating it could make it so. "I will not leave here without you."

She pressed her forehead to his inner thigh, and he felt her wet lashes against him, anointed by eyes that had teared from the strain of holding him.

"I cannot be yours, my lord, I have already told you so. I am Lord Zorac's."

"And I told you not to refer to him thus." He caught her face in gentle but firm fingers to show her his resolve. He saw hope fight with the desire raging through her and wanted it all to be for him. "You are eager for me to make your cunt weep again, are you not, milady?"

"Yes, my lord. It does so now."

"Is it me, or anyone who will do?" His fingers tightened, a warning to her tongue.

Lilith's dark eyes were a force of divine energy, so expressive and mysterious they were. "It is both, my lord. I cannot deny the need Zorac forces up in me, but I know, at this moment, if I have a choice, it is your touch alone I desire."

"Good." He rose, adjusting his clothes and controlling his dizziness from the force of his climax. She slid back awkwardly, giving him room, but remained on her knees, watching him with that tension in her face that told him she was again in the full grip of Zorac's pleasure-pain.

He squatted and lifted her in his arms. He carried her close, so he could feel her substance against his skin.

"You are too thin," he said softly. He brought her to the bed. When he had removed the damp brocade coverlet, he had exposed a pile of furs beneath. He saw bear, lion and wolf, all the predators, and a sheepskin. The lamb and the lion lay together in this bed. He saw a pelt he did not recognize, a pale soft fur, like a horse's winter coat, the color of glimmering moonlight and pale sun melting together. One edge was tasseled with a long silken mane, nearly a man's arm in length. It was as thick as Lilith's hair, but the threads were so fine it fell smooth like water and did not tangle where it lay on the bed.

He sat her upon that skin and gathered it on her shoulders. The long mane fell over her breasts, mixing with her own red locks, so she looked a creature of fire and moonlight. He went to the table to retrieve the bread, cheese and wine left for them.

"What is the animal that created such a coat?" He asked.

"It is a unicorn."

Thomas stopped in mid-motion, turned. "You are not jesting," he said.

She shook her head. She looked down at the skin, touched the soft fur. "Zorac used the horn to make a rare powder to protect the innocence of those he safeguards. It is how a man is pained if he touches Asneth wrongly, and how Elias never comes to harm, walking around in blindness."

He would sink to such vile behavior as to murder—"

"No, my lord," she spoke hastily. "I cannot allow you to believe that. My lord Zorac came upon the male unicorn, dying from a hunter's arrow. He had been lured by the touch of the hunter's virgin daughter. At the last minute the girl betrayed her father, overwhelmed by the good of the unicorn. She tried to warn the beast, to make him run from her, but an instant too late. The man wounded him mortally, but the unicorn fled into the woods, denying him his prize, and that is when Zorac found him."

Lilith stroked the fur curved around her hip. "Zorac stayed at the unicorn's side until he died, and told him he would take the horn and pelt to his home so no one else would take advantage of the creature's power. Their language is different from men, but the unicorn understood him, and Zorac could hear the beast's language in his heart.

"So you see," she said, "there is no evil in Zorac, except that which my actions have inspired."

It was as if the whole castle was a shrine to lost innocence, with his Great Whore trapped amid it all, taunted by what she could no longer be. Thomas swallowed his heated reaction to the sorrow in her voice and brought the bread and cheese to the bed. He put the wine on the floor and sat next to her.

She shrugged, attempting to wrest the coat off of her, and Thomas reached out and held it around her white shoulders, pressing it so that her arms pushed against her bare breasts, curving them together and lifting them for his appreciative gaze.

"Pure innocence is a lovely thing, my lady," he said. "But in men it only exists in untested form. And in that guise it is close kin to ignorance, and unintentional cruelty."

Something moved in her expression. Shock. Perhaps fear. Helene had taught him the virtues of patience. So rather than pressing the advantage, Thomas said simply, "Far safer for the unicorn to come lay its head in the lap of the man or woman who has learned the nature of suffering and regret. To my way of thinking, that is the more pure soul, even if less innocent."

"You will despise me in the end, my lord, and ride away as Zorac said."

She raised her face, her nostrils flaring as if she were taking in the scent of his heated skin, and her lips parted. It was an odd sensation, watching her body react so strongly to his, while so many thoughts, disconnected from the desire, apparently swirled in her mind.

"You are my lady. I embrace your darkness as well as your light. You belong to me, Lady Lilith," he tucked a hair behind her ear, smoothing over the shell shape. "Now, I want you on your stomach."

"You are commanding again, my lord."

"I am, and if you are wise, you will obey." There was a hint of a smile in his voice that seemed to startle her, and he managed to keep it there, though it angered him deeply that she had been denied an understanding of such a simple thing as intimate, teasing loveplay.

She turned onto one hip, and his hand came under her to help her with the turn where her own hands could not. Her dexterity without their balance spoke of how often Zorac kept her thus, but some maneuvers would require even more than the lean leg and stomach muscles she had developed.

He stopped her and slid the five bed pillows under her. They were overstuffed, so he had to raise her up, then lower her. He adjusted her forward, so that her thighs were forced open by the back width of the top pillow. Her breasts hung over the front edge, loose and wobbling. Her knees did not quite reach the mattress now, and she trembled, awkward and helpless, her cheek pressed against the mattress, her neck at an uncomfortable angle while her arse was tilted high in the air.

He brought a small stool from by the fire and placed it at her head, so she could lay her cheek against it to support her neck. Her head and neck now sloped down only a handspan lower than her shoulders. It was a vulnerable position, but no longer physically uncomfortable.

He sat back on the bed and extended a bite of the bread and cheese in his fingers. "Eat from my hand, my lady, and I will strengthen you for what lies ahead."

"I am content to go forward, my lord. My body fair screams it is so."

"But your body must be nourished by more than my seed, lady," he said. "The desire for simple sustenance has been drowned out by the cries of your mind for lustful excess. You need to ground your body with the nourishment of food, to know what your body truly desires. Eat."

She took it from his fingers, her lips as gentle and tentative as a foal, and she chewed. "You keep speaking as if I have a choice, my lord, to simply walk away from Zorac."

"Your body may not be able to resist his spell, my lady, for flesh responds to the strongest influence. However, your mind, properly reinforced, may be able to assert its own desires."

"You make it sound as if I can transform these carnal pleasures into a sacred ritual."

"Indeed, lady. Another." Her tongue touched his fingertips this time and he thought he might never let her take a bite of food again unless it came from his hand, to feel the caress of those lips. "Your mind is still strong. I see it in the way you look at Zorac, and at me. True pleasure is still possible for you, even amongst the pain and the lust he forces upon you."

"Your voice is as arousing to me as your hands, my lord," she whispered, drawing one of his fingers all the way into her mouth with the bread. "Please..."

Food could fuel the strength of the spell, he knew, and it appeared to be doing so, rapidly.

"My lord..." she breathed.

"Yes, Lilith?"

"This...it feels...I am so roused for you, but it is not as before. I feel Zorac's hand upon me, but these things you do to me, it is as if more than my...than the place between my legs is roused. It is as if you are catching my mind and soul on fire as well. I cannot bear it if you do not put your lance in me. I do not dread it. I need to be full of you, joined with you. I can bear the torture if you at least fill the empty part of me."

Her eyes raised to his, hungry and confused. "How is it I feel this way? Is this part of your spell?"

Thomas laid his palm on her temple. "I cannot yet, my lady. But it pleasures me deeply to hear your words. You begin to see me as your Master, instead of Zorac."

"But is not being your slave the same as being Zorac's, my lord?" Denied, her eyes flashed. "Why must I have a Master to free myself?"

"You mistake my meaning, lady, but perhaps soon you will understand it. I told you, a knight is purposeless without a liege lord to whom to pledge his sword. However, a knight sure of what he believes will choose his liege lord carefully. He chooses his master, and that is very important."

"But I am no knight. Why do I need a liege lord at all?"

He lifted the bread board by its thick wooden handle, brushing crumbs to the floor. "Because, my lady, you are mine. It is a simple truth, and you deny it only out of fear."

Lilith's eyes widened at the sight of the board, clutched like a weapon in his palm.

"My lord," her lips moistened as she pressed them together. "Surely you do not intend to beat me?"

"I do, my lady." He bent and gathered her hair in his hand, pushing its weight off her pale back and hips so the mass of it lay in a fiery tangle to the left of her shoulder. He felt her shiver beneath his touch. "What is more, you are going to like it."

He slid his hand down her back, over the smooth skin, the shallow channel of her spine.

"But, I...did I do something to displease you?"

"Not a thing, my lady. It is amazing, how a firm spanking focuses the mind on your Master, and brings forth the pleasure in you to serve him."

"You did not strike me as the type of man who enjoys abusing women," she said bitterly, turning her face away.

He knelt, turned her face back to him with an unrelenting hand. Their eyes were only inches apart, and his were steady and hot, certain that he was causing her breath to quicken for more reasons than Zorac's spell. "If you feel abused, lady," he said quietly, "when this is done, tell me so. I will allow you to do the same to me, on any part of my body you choose."

"I am afraid you will hurt me, my lord. You are a large man, and a strong one."

"Trust is what this is about, lady. There is a power to trust that can clarify your feelings more quickly than you expect." He stroked the broad end of the board against her rump and watched her fingers close into nervous fetal shapes. "You will feel pain, but the pleasure will be greater, I promise."

Lilith studied him from beneath her dark lashes. Her lips were pale pink and swollen from worrying them with her teeth, drawing the blood to them, the way he intended his words to draw the blood to the slick passages of her cunt.

"I trust you, my lord," she said at last. "But would you..." she stopped, her jaw tightening. Her eyes flashed with something like chagrin, mixed with embarrassment.

"What, my lady?" Thomas laid his hand along her neck, stretched out between the pillow and the stool. He could break it with a hard clasp of his hand, but he had learned that breaking precious things was terrifyingly easy. Creating, building and protecting were the things that took true strength. Of course, Zorac had not found it so easy to destroy Lilith. He had not reckoned on her resilience, which Thomas was counting on to save her.

"Will you...kiss me?"

He smiled. He bent forward, bracing the board on one luscious buttock. The kiss was an act of deep intimacy, much different from the most carnal act, and his lady had requested it from him. That made it, to him, their first true kiss. He stroked his fingers beneath her chin, fanned them out to frame her jaw and cheek, the tips just brushing the opening to her ear. She murmured, a soft whimper of pleasure. He went under the line of her hair, and it tickled his knuckles.

His lips touched hers and sensation shot through him, from mouth to chest to groin to feet and back again, a wild spiral so fast it shuddered across his skin like the wind upon a lake.

He parted her lips gently with his, touched her tongue with his own, traced her teeth, let the moisture from their two mouths join and excite. His grip slid to her throat and tightened there so he felt her pulse against his hand, as if he held a bird. A bird who could soar far above man and yet be crushed in a careless fist. Her helplessness was a deep pull in his stomach, the knowledge that she must simply experience what he could do to pleasure her.

He pulled back just a breath and stared into her eyes, his knuckles rubbing up and down the cord of her throat.

"One day, my lady, I will spend a full day doing just this, from your first sight of sunrise, to when your eyes fall shut against the onset of night." He rubbed his cheek against the flushed heat of hers. "I will wake you in the morning with kisses and I will kiss you all day. In our bed, at breakfast, in your garden, in your bath. Short, gentle kisses, just bare touches of your mouth with mine. Long, deep ones that will loosen your thighs because you will unconsciously desire to be fucked as deeply there as I am penetrating your mouth.

"But I will do naught but kiss you, even as you beg me to do more. I will make love only to your mouth in all the ways you wish me to make love to your body."

"My lord," she murmured, unable to stop her body from performing sinuous rolls at his words. He wanted to slake his thirst with the perspiration that covered her skin, rather than take another drink of water again. "Please."

"Please, what, lady?" he asked softly.

"Please, do as you said you will. I ache for your touch, even if it is only through the strike of this board."

"Your will is my desire, lady."

Thomas rose, shifted the paddle in his hand and lay his palm on her tense back. He admired the white curves propped high before him, like the perfect softness of pale yeast loaves pressed together in the hearth, and the line that divided them and concealed other mysterious places. The board whispered over her buttocks, and she made a soft sound.

He slapped her bottom, a light stroke with the wood. She jumped, but he could see the lack of pain relaxed her. He did it again, several times, getting her used to the sensation, and enjoying the way the slender back arched and shoulders tightened, the bite down on her bottom lip. She was widening her legs, raising herself to meet his stroke, exposing her wetness to him. Her breath became harsh.

He caught her, sliding a hand beneath her hips next time she raised them. He lifted her body above the pillows. He brought the paddle down in earnest, and she cried out. His next stroke delivered a stinging blow to those sensitive blood-filled folds. Her sex looked like a dark red peach, running with juices.

She cried out again, but he kept on, watching fair snow turn to a rosy blush, and feeling his own reaction grow and swell to painful proportions. Her breath came in a sob now.

"My lord,...it is so much worse, please..."

Her cunt was indeed rippling in the near orgasm that Zorac permitted her. Thomas was heightening the sensations, driving her mad with unrelieved desire. He watched, fascinated despite himself, as the rippling became a continuous spasm. Lilith's head jerked and her teeth scraped the wood of the stool. She gnawed like an animal losing its mind from the pain of a trap. Her legs kicked out helplessly against Thomas's strength, and her arousal was as strong a scent as perfumed oil.

Forgive me, lady. But I must do this to you. I promise I shall make it up to you, if God makes me worthy enough to free you.

"Hold, my lady," he murmured, and lowered his paddle to the bed. He kept her in the air with his one arm.

"No..." she fought him like a berserker. She was unable to twist around with his hold on her, but still she tried, rearing up to try and flip herself over, too far gone to accept there was nothing such a motion would gain her.

He turned her over on her back, so she was stretched out on the pillows, her back arched, her breasts the highest part of her, like fertile hills down a smooth, sloping expanse of stomach. He spread and re-manacled her legs, and with her arms bound to her sides, she was unable to do more than rock herself back and forth, and keen in that soft, breathy voice that slid down his back like the touch of her hands.

He studied the soft curls between her legs and the columns of her thighs, a landscape he would be content to contemplate until the Earth her body invoked in his mind crumbled away and left them all adrift in the Mother's Womb once more.

She drew deep breaths, trying to calm herself, though her eyes on him were far from calm. They had the hunger of the succubus. He bent to his saddlebags, withdrew the carved box that had revealed his intent to Zorac, and opened it.

The phallus had been formed from the soft, sucking clay of a cave deep in the earth. It had been gathered by the hands of the faithful, priests and priestesses of the Old Ways. The clay had been molded over the cock of one of the priests and painted upon the breasts and mons of the High Priestess Helene. They had joined with each other thus, in the ritual that brought together the incarnation of the Goddess and the Horned One, lord of sun.

When the ritual was complete, the anointed clay had been carefully removed from each of them, molded, fired and glazed into the smooth and sacred object he held now, containing the fluids of their passion and Creation.

Thomas believed in God, had fought in the name of His Son, but after his time with the priestesses, he found no conflict in accepting the truths of the Old Ways as well. What was in his hands was holy, and he intended to use it for a sacred purpose.

He lifted the polished phallic object so Lilith could see it. "I roused you with fire and water, my lady. Earth and air will complete a circle about your soul. These four elements are greater than man or magician."

He cupped the side of her face in his hand. She turned into his touch, her eyes closing, her face rigid with the torment of her unreleased pleasure. He lifted the curved sculpture of earth. He found her opening with his thumb, stroked through the soaked lips as she cried out in anguish, and parted them with the head of the large, smooth phallus. He kept his thumb over that sweet jewel that guarded her gateway, preventing contact between it and the tool of the ritual.

The cock was larger than a normal man, but curved for her shape. He took his time. Her eyes opened again, this time showing a trace of uncertainty.

"You can take all of it, my lady," he murmured soothingly. "I know you can." He eased it in an inch, then two, stretching her, feeling her juices coat it, further lubricate it for entry.

The chains of the manacles could be adjusted to spread her legs wider, and Thomas did so now, one-handed, though Lilith protested in an incoherent moan.

"We go wider, lady," he commanded, with gentle sternness. "Spread yourself for me."

Her thighs slid away from each other, further exposing what lay between them. Thomas swallowed at the sight of the pink nether lips gripping the large organ, feeling a sympathetic strong contraction in his own. He growled when she lifted her hips and showed him the tracks of arousal on the inside of her legs. He kept his hands steady though his heart was not, and pushed the lance in half way. She whimpered and his gaze shifted in concern, but her head had fallen back on the pillows and her mouth was open, drawing in air, her teeth bared as she gasped. The tiny bud of flesh beneath his thumb throbbed and she screamed. He put his hand to the side of her head and her teeth sank hard into the callused Venus mound of his hand.

She convulsed, her hips jerking savagely for a release he was denying her. He slid the smooth brown cock all the way home.

He hated drawing out her anguish thus, but the priestess's instructions had been thorough and precise. By the blessed Virgin, he had never been so hard in his life and not come. He could feel his seed leaking against his belly beneath his clothes. Lilith's eyes were on his cock, straining against the fabric of his hose. Her nostrils flared as if she could smell it.

"I can bear no more,...my lord," she said. The plaintive whisper wrenched his heart as much as her tears, which were falling from her eyes to the pillows.

"It must stay thus, for just another moment, lady. You

must submit to its presence inside you, accept it being there, before I can proceed to grant you release."

She choked. "It is inside me, my lord."

"It is not that which I mean. You must become still, accepting it as a wild mare accepts the bridle of her Master and stands, eager to run wild but awaiting his will. You must be still, my lady, to hear the will of more than your own flesh."

"It is easy for you to say, my lord," she said on a harsh gasp, "when you do not have to endure it."

"Aye, lady, so it is." He cupped his palm over her feverish temple, touching the fine hairs close to her scalp, even as he kept his other hand on the phallus, and his thumb in place. "But when a man is wounded on the battlefield, there is a moment that comes, long hours afterward. You move past the agonizing pain, into an acceptance of the abhorrent trauma to your flesh. All senses of the body become dull, and yet the things of the spirit, your desires and perceptions, become clearer than anything you have ever experienced. It is a terrible and yet miraculous thing, for it often heralds the end. For you, it will be the end of your life here. Not your death," he assured her. "I will not allow you to leave me."

"Where?" she asked. "Where did such a thing happen to you?"

He pulled aside the fabric of his tunic so she could see the scar, the long gash of a battle axe, embedded over his heart.

She startled him by lifting her upper body. He aided her with a hand beneath her shoulders. He was not sure of her intent, but then she pressed her lips to that scar. His heart hitched in his chest.

Though her body blazed with heat from her passion, her breasts heaving erratically against his chest, her thighs trembling, her kiss was a tender one. She kept her mouth on his scar, motionless, and her lips felt like the touch of feathers.

She stayed in that position for awhile, saying nothing, her jaw pressed against the skin revealed by the opening of his tunic, her lashes fanning her cheeks so he could not see her eyes. He held her against him with one arm, his other holding the phallus still within her. He wished he could hold her cradled in his lap.

Her body's jerks eased at length, and he watched as she once again exercised a control over the uncontrollable that astounded and humbled him.

"I could have lost you in that moment," she said, her eyes lifting to meet his.

"You did not."

She stared at him, tears leaking from her dark eyes like tiny crystallized souls fleeing the horror of the abyss.

"My lord,...if this does not work, I beg you, please, take my life. I care not if I go to dust and oblivion. I am so tired, it would be as much heaven as I could want, and more than I deserve, I am sure."

Thomas caught her tears on his fingertips. "I know you think of yourself at the end of your strength, Lilith," he said. "I have pushed you hard. I feel your body roused to pain beneath my hands. But you have strength, and the end is so close. Inside the circle I will form about you, you will find the answer to your freedom, know it in your heart. Trust me, as you trusted me just now, to understand the nature of pleasure and pain together."

"You do not know what crime I have committed. I may not be worthy of this ritual, and you may not want me if you knew."

"That does not matter," he rebuked her, holding her close to him, her bare breasts pushed up against his broad chest, her softness the only pillow he would ever desire again. "You look into my eyes and see the other part of you, as I see the other part of me. I have sought you in my dreams, whether it is on the cold, bloodsoaked ground of a fresh battlefield, or the comfort of my bed, which I desire to share with you. You are my quest, the quest of my life, Lilith. I came not for the glory of God, or the desire to make a name for myself. I came for you."

"But Zorac said,...you serve the cause of Arthur."

"I, like many before me, have served Arthur's cause, and will do so, always. But he knew men and women make their own choices. His love for his two closest friends destroyed him but it also resurrected him. He honored the love they bore him, and for each other, until the end. It will always be a hard world with hard choices, lady. Men will be selfish and cruel, except in the cause of love. That is the one charge for which they will sacrifice everything. That is the cause I serve, though it has taken me many years to understand that."

He straightened. "Now, my lady, no more tears. You have accepted this cock within your tight opening, and now there is more."

He eased her back to the pillows and took his hands away from her, leaving the phallus seated deep within her.

"You must hold it within you, my lady. That is my command."

From the same elaborately carved box, he withdrew a purple feather with tiny beaded tips. The beads were so light they did not weigh down the strand on which each rested. He fitted the stem of the feather into a tiny slot just beneath the curved handle of the phallus. Lilith stiffened as the slight draft in the room, and the act of seating the feather, stroked the tips against that tight nub of flesh his thumb no longer guarded.

Thomas moved so he stood at the foot of the bed, gazing down the loveliness of her body from between her knees.

She tried to lift her head from the slight downward slope of the stool, but he made a gesture and she settled back, looking at him awkwardly from beneath her lashes.

"In a minute, I shall open the window," he pointed just beyond him, "and the night breeze will come through. The feather will begin to do its gentle dance on you, and render you helpless before the power of the slightest touch of air. You will concentrate on nothing beyond the build of pleasure in your cunt. You will feel your juices rising and the power of the Earth growing within you."

"My lord—"

"No, no words now," he commanded softly. "Ride it, Lilith. Hold it as if it is my lance you grasp with your muscles of silk. I challenge you not to call my name as you explode with your release. You will not be able to stop yourself."

"And you fancy yourself a magician now, able to command my words," she spat, her body's ache spiraling her back to anger again.

"I am your Master, and your love, and your heart. Soon, you will not be able to deny the truth of it, no more than you will be able to resist squeezing the phallus with your own muscles, work it deeper within you. Your body has the strength to serve its own desires."

Her chin lifted, her eyes flashing defiance. The tremble of her lips clearly suggested the turmoil within. He loved her, loved watching her pride fight her desire.

He rose, his gaze never leaving her, and moved to the window. The latch turned easily, well-oiled and maintained by Zorac's staff. Zorac had obviously never feared she would take her own life. Or perhaps he had not cared. A shadow darkened Thomas's eyes as he considered that Zorac had hoped to drive her to a damnation of her soul. Then he would have been spared the energy of torturing her. He could simply have contemplated her burning in hell forever. Let the Devil do his work.

Thomas took a deep breath. Anger had no place in this moment. He pushed the window open and felt the night air touch his face. The moon was rising in the sky, and there were stars, so many that they were a blaze of jewels, a good omen. The breeze from the nearby sea pushed against his chest and he stepped aside, giving it its way.

It swept into the room, riffling the heavy tapestries on the walls. The fire leaped in a flickering pattern. He heard a soft gasp and turned his head toward the bed.

There were things of beauty in the world. He had seen many of them, some of them ironically in the most horrible of circumstances. But he could not think of anything more beautiful in all his travels than what he saw on the bed.

His lady, his beautiful Lilith, her body arched high atop a mountain of pillows, her thighs spread, the muscles within her cunt tight, keeping the lance deep within her. Her white stomach an expanse of milk and satin. The crease of flesh where the weight of her breasts lay on her ribs, the pale curves trembling with her erratic breathing. The column of her throat, arched back and exposed as she gasped for air. Her body jerked, small motions, as the wind caught hold of the feathers and swept their beaded tips over her drenched petals. The motion was like a soft rain, unpredictable in where the drops would fall, but relentless in their determination to soak the earth.

He moved softly, not wishing to distract her, not wanting to change the picture in any way unless it was her desire that changed it.

The earthen lance moved, and Thomas's mouth became dry as he saw her wet lips tighten on the shaft, pull it into herself slightly and then ease it back that same amount with the muscle release. She would not move it further than that, with her thighs spread so far open, but that small movement would focus the friction of the head on the place within her that the curved edge of the lance was designed to seat against. The priestess had told him it was a place of intense pleasure to a woman.

He wished her hands were free so he could bind them in her soft hair, wrap the strands around her crossed wrists beneath her to arch her body up even further, displaying her more tautly to his pleasure. That would be a joy he would anticipate for another time.

He wanted to be close to her. He needed to touch her now more than he needed air, but he stayed where he was, just watching her, his heart pounding, aching, knowing the rest was up to her.

Chapter Four

Lilith had thought, so many times that it became one of the mantras she used to keep from losing her mind, that if she ever freed herself, she would eschew bodily pleasures forever and commit herself to a convent.

She knew only the pain of unrelenting lust, its savage tearing, its debasing need. She had never felt a woman's desire, as Thomas called it, this physical desire coupled with emotional need, this strong, overwhelming need for intimacy with one man. The ability, not only to join with him, but to crawl inside of him and merge with his flesh.

She had discovered much about herself over the past five years. She had learned that almost anything could be endured, and that hatred could give the body strength to survive. She had cried her share of tears into the unicorn's pelt, but it had been some time since Zorac had won the privilege of seeing them.

Her body was being consumed by the elements Thomas had invoked. She felt every naked inch of her flesh, that creation of dust that became so much more with the spirit to animate it. Fire licked over her skin and she wondered if it had leaped from the hearth and covered her with rippling, silken fingers. Moisture covered her beneath the cloak of fire, and gathered between her legs, soaking the object that impaled her. Her muscles acted against her will, milking it within her, sliding it that small, excruciating bit, forward and back.

He was there, larger than life, a shadow in her consciousness. His intent stillness, his focus solely for her, stoked that fire.

She was used to the futile build to peak and dreaded hanging there, like Zorac had described it, a convict condemned to hang in a state of eternal suffocation. This was a different feeling.

The first time, with the water, it had taken her by surprise. Now, she knew that delicious feeling was coming again, but it was taking her higher than before, lifting her spirit as well as her body. The height was beginning to frighten her. Every muscle of her body was gathering, as if preparing for an impact it might not survive, and yet she was splayed open, so vulnerable, when everything in her screamed that she should shield herself.

When Zorac had brought her here, she had no experience, no understanding of the knife edge of arousal he had invoked within her. In her ignorance, there were no shields to protect her from her body's responses. She had no control. Zorac had allowed her free rein around the castle and she had flung herself upon guardsmen who were strangers. She had wrapped her legs around them and undulated shamelessly against their cocks while they laughed. As each guardsmen bore her to the rushes to thrust into her, it heightened her raw desire. When one man relieved his own need, the next took his place. In the end, she rolled on the dirty floor, half-mad, her hands seeking herself, rubbing herself furiously for something, she knew not what. Her hands were wrenched away. In those first days, she was often chained up on the table, like a rabid dog, to buck in a sensual display for the pleasure of the guardsmen. A gag silenced her wails of confusion and need. Zorac watched her ignorant distress with a look of grim satisfaction.

She had learned then what true hatred was, and that she had pride that existed beyond childish vanity and self-pity. She learned to suffer her body's torment in silence, to fight her desire to rub and fornicate every second until exhaustion granted her a few moments of sleep. She learned it was tolerable if she was able to be still. Movement of any kind made it worse. Walking, the rubbing together of one's thighs, sitting where one's privates were in contact with a cushion, all those were things to be avoided.

She grew paler and thinner, but she grew proportionately stronger in will. The fire of hatred that fueled her rose into her eyes and burned there, so the guardsmen, while not averse to fucking her, rarely met her gaze.

She found her shields. She could not stop the desire from wracking her body ceaselessly, but now Zorac had to go to extra efforts to reduce her to those levels. She had no illusions. He could do it. Sometimes he pushed her that far, just to show her he could, but he seemed satisfied knowing how much effort she had to devote to keeping the slightest amount of dignity for herself.

Zorac had thought to punish her further with Thomas, as he had punished her by using her for the entertainment of his guests in the past. But Thomas was different.

She could no longer hold her shields in place. It was as if the first climax had shattered them, cleansed her with those purifying elements of fire and water to prepare her for this, this plunge into the primitive grasp of dark earth and howling winds. Her body arched higher, and still her passions were stoked, the phallus rubbing her in tiny, sinuous circles on a place inside that would destroy her when it exploded. Her thighs spread wide, straining against the manacles, working it, and the earthen lance thrust in deeper, rasping against her silken walls. The wind rose outside, and she cried out, a guttural cry, as the feathers picked up their dance, every touch a diamond spark against quivering, sensitive flesh.

"Thomas, my lord," she gasped. "Thomas..."

His name gave her an anchor, and he was there, at her head, by her side, kneeling where she could see him. He was so beautiful. She wondered if he knew that, how his amber eyes and copper hair enhanced a strong, sensual face that no woman would ever forget. And as if that were not enough, he had been blessed with a lean, muscular body that seemed quite capable of serving a woman's every need, whether it be from her heart or body. And he was hers, wasn't he? Didn't he say so? Why did she resist the thought?

"We may not touch, my lady, not yet," he murmured. "Though I dearly wish to do so. But I am here. Do not be afraid. Let every shield fall, and give yourself to me."

How had he known? She suddenly, desperately wanted to reach out to him, could not bear it if he moved away. She was afraid to do this alone, without his touch. Her mind was no longer able to think of anything that had sustained her until now. Not pride, not hatred. All that was mutable, but there was Thomas. Thomas was somehow eternal. She could almost see the light of him shining through the earthly skin and bone as she spiraled higher. The body would wither away in time, but the light would remain, would always be there to warm her, guide her.

A gust of wind loosed the shutter and the hard clap, along with the burst of erratic air, stroked the feather across her gate. Her thighs yanked back against her chains as if she was about to give labor, driving the phallus hard into her.

The light from Thomas exploded, blinding her, consuming her. The climax rolled over her with the power of the ocean thundering just beyond the castle. She felt as if the energy detonating from within her could have called the sea to rise up over the diminutive structure of Zorac's castle, crash over and through it, drowning them all.

She suddenly could see herself through Thomas's eyes, her body immersed in sensuality, her breasts thrust up as rigid as mountains from the slopes of the earth herself, her hair spread like fire upon the unicorn's pelt. Her dark eyes were onyx embedded with amber, and her slim fingers clutched the pelts she wished were the secure anchor of his skin and muscle.

She was helpless as an infant, and she gave a cry of terror and loss.

I shall not survive this.

I am here, Lilith. I am here.

Her breasts were impossibly full. They would have spilled over the cup of Thomas's large palm, and she could imagine them there, caressed by his long fingers. Her cunt was spilling honey over the contours of the cock inside her, onto her thighs, soaking the fur beneath her.

The cry escalated into a scream, the movements of her hips pumping her impossibly higher. The feather licked her like a wet mouth, the wind its breath, playing in among the saturated fronds.

Her sweating body formed a bridge, rising up in a graceful arch from the pillows. She was still screaming. The pleasure was tearing her, taking her on a ride like a galloping horse, rushing for a cliff. The stallion flung itself into the air. It tumbled her into a glittering stillness of white light and final, powerful silence.

I can take no more.

I am here, my lady, my own...

Thomas, my lord...

§

She was floating in that whiteness. There was no form or shape to the world around her. It was peaceful, still, the whiteness given texture by drifts like clouds traveling through the air around her, touching her skin with the kiss of fog-like mist.

Had she died? No, she knew she could not be dead. Somehow the ritual had taken her here. Perhaps this was the sacred circle of which he had spoken. Perhaps she was unconscious and dreaming.

She heard laughter, unkind laughter coming from the throat of a girl she knew, and her heart stilled. She turned, and the mist lifted a few paces away, as if she had the front seat for a stage play.

She looked at herself as she had been five years before, a prettier version, with a voluptuous body and no lines of pain or dark shadows in those bright brown eyes.

Her younger self stood before a young man with a fall of blonde hair and an earnest, somewhat scholarly face. He knelt to her.

"What may I do for you, my lady, to prove my love?"

"No," Lilith whispered. She felt Thomas here, behind her, and did not want him to see, but she could not turn, could do nothing but watch.

The girl looked at her hand, clasped in that of her suitor,

and considered. She blushed modestly, but Lilith saw the bored annoyance beneath the flirtatious lashes. It was so obvious, she wondered the young man did not see it.

Many of the young men pursuing the ideal of courtly love had gotten more obsessed with their flowery phrases than the women they claimed inspired them. But if she had only known how to look, through the eyes of experience and wisdom, she would have seen that this boy meant them deeply, even if his passion obscured the mettle of the woman to whom he said them.

"Prove your love to me in arms, my lord. Take yourself far away, to the service of Christendom and our country, on the borders. Die with my name on your lips."

Her voice was so gentle in its mockery, he never heard the acid undertones. Lilith wanted to believe she hadn't meant it, but she knew the truth was worse than if she *had* meant it. She hadn't cared whether she meant it or not. She had simply wanted him gone.

He stood, keeping her hand. Lilith's fingers fluttered, remembering her desire to pull free, get away.

"Your wish, my lady, is my only desire. Grant me a token of yours to give me strength and to send back to you when I have proven my love to you."

She didn't care for the necklace she wore anyway. It was a gift from her aunt, who had the taste of a stable hand. This was a good way to be done with it. The young Lilith put it on his neck, accepted with barely contained impatience his fervent thanks, and turned away. She did not bother to watch him leave.

The older Lilith watched the young man. He pressed his lips to the garish medallion of her necklace, touched with wonder the skin of his neck where she had touched him when she placed it on him. He had been so young, but she realized he had likely had no more years than she had now. She felt centuries older than he had ever been.

Hot tears stung her eyes and she reached out a hand, but the boy was gone. She recoiled as another stepped through his melting apparition. Zorac, with the same blue eyes as his younger brother, only his eyes and mouth were hard with grief.

The wizard strode to the younger Lilith, where she played with her friends in the solar. He spoke his introduction and extended the necklace. "My brother sends this to you as proof of his love."

Lilith watched herself take it, visibly try to remember who this man's brother might be. She shrugged, assessed the value of the gift she also did not recognize, then laid it aside. She used the moment to assess the potential of the messenger beneath her lashes and found him to her liking. She smiled up at Zorac in practiced innocent flirtation. The expression died before the rage that swept over his grief-ravaged face.

The images wavered and dissipated in the mist, and Lilith stood, staring at where they had been. She had lived portions of those two scenes over in her mind so many times. This time it was so real, it allowed her no place to hide from any moment of it. She could offer no apologies, could not beg for forgiveness, for her crime had been so great, she did not have the right to do either.

"How may I prove my love to you, lady?"

Like a warm wave of tears that passed through her entire body, his voice spoke to her.

Lilith turned.

Thomas stood ten paces away, but in this dream reality, his words were against her ear.

He was naked, as she was, and she drew in her breath at the fineness of him. Strong limbs, thighs and arms covered by a light mat of hair that gleamed with the same copper highlights of his hair. His proud cock was aroused and thick. She looked at it and it was as if her eyes were intimately connected to all the nerves of her body, for she could feel what it would be like to have the broad shaft of that cock against her dripping sex. She could feel it push in between the walls of flesh and claim its sovereignty in that dark, moist castle.

She had never felt that way about any man, not under Zorac's spell, not ever. He was here, in her world of sorrow, stillness and shame. He did not come to condemn her, or exonerate her, but to stand at her side. His lips and eyes reflected his love and gentleness.

Perhaps it was the purifying steps of the ritual he had taken, perhaps it was some magic she did not understand. However, the pride he had roused in her to resist his claim melted away. She was here in this space, just Lilith, and she needed him in her life, more than she would ever need anything again.

"I am not worthy of your love," she said, her voice as small as she felt herself to be.

"That is for me to decide, lady. How may I prove my love to you?"

She faced him, two beings as bare and alone as the day Adam and Eve faced one another in Eden, God's presence a mist around them.

"Be my Master," she said, "and never leave me."

She moved then. It was ten steps to reach him, and when she got there, his arms were open. She moved into them and him, pressing all of herself against him. She choked on her emotions as she realized she could raise her arms, wrap them around his hard waist, and hold him as close as he was holding her.

"How will I prove myself to you, my lord?" She spoke into his chest.

"You need do nothing, my lady, but be who you are."

She could not dare to trust the simplicity of that, but in his arms, here, it felt possible. "Will you kiss me?" she asked, as she had before, on a more earthly plane. She was seized with the fear this was a dream, and she would wake and none of it would have happened.

"I will do much more than that, Lady," he said, his head bending to reach her upturned face. "It is time, now that you have accepted me, to make you mine in truth."

Before she could reply to that, his lips were upon hers, and all the hard urgency she had seen him bank within himself as he prepared her for the ritual now poured into that kiss.

His palms slid down her bare arms, cupping her elbows, drawing her in so her breasts were on his chest. His cock pressed in a hot and insistent way against her, almost comforting in its demand, the wet tip making a line of need across her skin. Her hands clutched his sides, tracing the bottom of his ribs, wondering which was the empty spot where God had given one from man to woman, to join them forever.

"Your mouth, lady," he murmured. "Open it to mine, as you will your moist cunt to my lance, in due time."

She obeyed, and his tongue found hers, stroked, thrust and made her open wider, press more tightly to him, and keen deep in her throat, her fingers digging into his skin.

Yes. More.

He broke the kiss, turned her with irresistible strength so her back was against him, and he could caress her at will, explore her body as she rested against him, secure in the circle of his arm, his cheek pressed against her hair.

He did not explore her in the way she expected, touching her in those places men were wont to touch. He molded his palms to her shoulders, feeling the structure of the bones pressing into his hands. He slid his grip down her arms, and she could feel the sensation, every inch, because of how slowly he did it, learning her, as she learned to accept his touch upon her. He curled his knuckles, followed the indentation of her ribs down to the flare of her hips.

He was destroying her with his soft caress. Everything inside her trembled, as if her heart itself was capable of tears. His thigh pressed against her buttock and leg and she turned her head, pressing her jaw against his chest as he continued his exploration. He moved his fingers forward, down the curve of her stomach. He lifted his touch from her, just a breath away, and raised the fine hairs of her flesh with the heated aura of his fingertips. Her hips lifted and he made a soothing noise in her ear to settle her down.

"This is difficult, my lord," she whispered against his skin as the white mist of this sacred plane curled around them. "It hurts." Her chest and stomach were aching with something that felt like a wound.

His lips brushed the back of her neck, and his arms came all the way around her, one across her chest, just above her breasts, the other about her waist, his fingers splayed out on the point of her shoulder and hip.

A quiet sob, like the sigh of a fawn in a hidden glade, escaped her lips. He held her like that in silence for awhile, letting her feel his heart beat against her shoulder blades, his cock pulse against the small of her back. The taut strength of his thighs, the heat of his chest and stomach against her skin, the movement of his breath against her neck and ear. She felt the white mist roll around them, a blanket shutting out everything but each other and that heart thudding against her. She was weeping, and she did not know why.

"You will have to choose once more, Lilith," his voice spoke through her. "You're almost free, but you must be willing to make a choice, believe you have the right to do so, in the world we have left."

She knew he was right, but did not want to face it yet, for she might make the wrong choice, and this would be the last moment of peace she might know again. She knew there was not another Thomas in the world for her.

As if he could read her thoughts, he pressed his lips to her throat, using a hint of teeth at first, and then deepening the bite. He did not break the skin but he pressed down hard, marking her in a way she felt tingle to the tips of her breasts and deep within her cunt. She swallowed, and made to turn, but he held her still, cupping her breasts, and ran his fingers over them like the touch of air.

"Speak your Master's name," he said, soft.

"Thomas,...my lord."

It came to her lips before she thought it. It was there, as easy to her as her own name. He had been right, what they were to each other. It made her so terribly afraid, the stark truths of this place where nothing could be hidden, against the reality of the world to which she must return, where her sanity depended on what she could hide.

It was one thing to obey Zorac by force, another to choose in this way. She realized how little she had given to the wizard. Her body and her hatred were such a little part of the person she was. He was her jailer, not her Master. A Master wanted what Thomas wanted. A total surrender, no secrets, no shields, nothing between them, spirit meeting spirit.

He turned her in his arms, his eyes intent and burning with the strong light of stars. "I see you still need convincing, my lady," he said. "Put your arms around my neck."

She obeyed, lifting arms that felt as weak as the day she was birthed to his shoulders, and curled them there as he eased her up to her toes, pulling her in to him. He lifted her. She gasped as he effortlessly, and with precision, sheathed his cock deep into her, his hand coming down to the plate of bone just above her buttocks to hold her firmly seated, the other arm around her back.

It was like the moment of Creation itself, an astounding sensation that catapulted her body's nerve centers into screaming ecstasy and curious stasis all at once. It was not the perilous edge Zorac had made her ride. This was a sudden sense of utter belonging, of wholeness, that could never lose its sense of wonder. Her senses had known chaos and instability for so long. Now those senses rushed to embrace this wholeness, bond to it in the desperate hope that it never be taken away again.

Dear God, he was right. He was her Master.

"Thomas." She said his name.

She lifted her head so they were eye to eye, and his lips brushed hers, his tongue tracing moisture on her dry lips. Her legs had accommodated his entry, wrapping around his hips, her heels brushing the tops of his muscular thighs, and now she thought she felt her heart beat in time with the throbbing organ impaling her.

"You are sweet, dear lady, so sweet," he said hoarsely. "It is like coming home to the Earth herself and finding rest and passion at once. I want to hear you scream my name."

He pressed his hand against her back, pushing her deeper onto him, and the reaction shot straight up into her chest.

He did it again, rocking his hips so she heard the wet, sucking noise of her eager sex gripping him as it had never gripped a man before. Its urgency came from its desire to be pleasured, and an equal desire to stay joined forever, as if her life and all its functions depended on it.

"Lilith," he murmured, and thrust again, the muscles of

his powerful shoulders rippling beneath her fingers. "Lilith," he said, his voice becoming deeper, more primitive. And thrust again.

Surely there had to be magic in this place, for she was certain his movements were causing the walls of her cunt to erupt into flame. Lilith struggled, not sure why she was struggling. Each shove of his hips pressing her thighs wider and penetrating her was pushing her out of hell, into the sweet air of the world again. His grip on her was ruthless, holding her hips still, not allowing her any movement. She simply had to bear the rub of his broad shaft within and without her as he withdrew, pumped forward, withdrew, each stroke a slow building fire across the tinder of her quivering flesh.

"I like the way you breathe, my lady, when I am fucking you so hard and well," he grunted. "You gasp each time my lance stretches you wide and buries inside you. I will hear that scream, Lilith."

She squeezed her eyes shut and buried her moan into his shoulder. His hands shifted, gripping both cheeks of her buttocks and opening her. He showed no signs of tiring, a man who carried pounds of armor into battle. She drank in his smell, felt the heat of his skin on her lips, and the need he roused in her turned savage. If he would be her Master, he could earn it, for she would be no meek servant, but a match for his strength.

She latched her teeth onto his shoulder with a growl, her passion bringing flashes of light and color to the inside of her lids, and now his blood on her tongue, mingling with her own saliva. She dug her nails into him, feeling the tough skin give way before her claws, and still he showed no sign of flagging.

"Fight me all you want, lady," he said, "I will not be denied your scream."

"My lord, let me—"

"No, Lilith," his voice was a groan against her throat. "You may draw blood from me, but you will take all of me within yourself. Feel my cock, and know it has the right to your cunt, as much as you have the right to my blood. I will not let you go."

The double meaning was not lost on her, but the white world was swirling into color around them, mist driven back by fire that would surely consume them. Color would take them back to reality, and she was afraid.

Her nipples rasped against the rough hair of his chest each time he brought her body against his with a powerful smack of flesh, the friction unable to be contained. He made her body shake with the force of his assault, the long, torturous slide of his lance all the way out, and back in again. Her muscles clenched him, tried to keep him deep within her, but he would drive her insane with this slow build to a climax that eliminated all her resistance to the truth of who he was to her, no matter what plane they were on.

She could hold her grip on him no longer. She reared back, her fingers slipping away, but his strength held her up. His head plunged down, his hot mouth capturing her nipple and half of her breast, licking, chewing, suckling her.

Lilith shrieked, convulsing at the strike of sensation that shot from that aroused nipple to her wetness. Her reaction gushed from her, too violent to be satisfied with a slippery impression of dampness, the usual discreet evidence of the volcanic spiritual and physical eruption of a woman in climax.

His name was on her lips, there waiting to be spoken again, to call him to her, bind him to her, as much as it bound her to him. It felt like her chest was tearing in two. Her heart screamed what it knew, her fear battling it to silence. Then she turned and saw his eyes, no more than a breath from hers, and there was nothing left to fear or fight.

Say it, Lilith. His voice was just a whisper in her heart, when she expected a shout.

"Master," she said. Then she screamed it, an urgent sound of pain and release at once, a wound torn open. The infection poured out, exposing all her hopes, impurities and fears in one moment, in that one word.

He held her, his lance pounding into her like a siege ram. Knocking down every defense, resounding within the echoing walls of her spirit, filling it with a promise, a possession. She felt him explode, a hot stream that made her cry out anew, her voice blending with his in their mutual surrender to one another, and his ragged breath chanting her name against her ear.

The white and colors came together, merging into darkness, until there was just a tinge of rose, like the light of the sun behind closed eyelids.

§

It was light behind closed eyelids. Firelight. Lilith slowly opened her eyes.

She was on the bed. Thomas held her in one strong arm while he gently cleaned her with a washcloth with his other hand. She watched him for a few moments, cozening her as he would a child. His copper hair fell softly over his forehead and bare shoulders, and his amber eyes glowed with the colors of firelight. As her ability to use her faculties returned and her nerve endings untangled enough to feel his touch upon her, it hit her like a warm slap of the sun that she was feeling his touch in languorous enjoyment.

Languorous, sated enjoyment. Her body trembled under his touch, but it was an emotional response, not a physical one. She had been satisfied. She, just as any woman after coitus, lay quiet under her lover's touch, wanting to touch him for the sake of intimacy, the remembrance of passion, and in anticipation of it, not the immediate demand for it.

She wanted to touch him. Her hand jerked up awkwardly, because she expected the bindings, and there were none. She hesitated, her hand in mid-air, afraid to move it further.

"It is gone," she whispered.

"I know." His fingers parted the lips of her cunt as he rubbed the cloth against her. She made a soft noise.

"I thought it was,...only there, that you and I..."

"The ritual of awakening took our minds there. Inside this sacred circle, our bodies obeyed what our spirits did elsewhere, so strong was its pull."

She got the courage to move her hand then. She raised unsteady fingers to his face, and he turned his attention to her. Beautiful eyes he had, and her fingers pressed on his lips, feeling their texture.

"You are angry with me, my lord?"

His brows drew together. "No, my lady. Why would you think it so?"

"You are so...quiet," she ventured. "I thought, perhaps, I displeased you in some way."

Thomas smiled, easing her heart, and he kissed her fingers. Done with his cleaning, he kept the warmth of the cloth over her tender opening, the heel of his hand pressed firmly there between her open legs, as if reminding her of his claim to her as much as soothing the tenderness his entry had caused, reassuring her further. She noticed he wore his hose and nothing else, so she could see the hair on his chest, the gleaming line of his shoulders. She noticed the elegant lines of the muscles in his legs, the bulge of his genitals straining the snug fit of the cloth. She noticed because she, Lilith, *wanted* to notice these things.

"I once thought," she managed, "that I would convince my father to marry me to a malleable older man of wealth. I thought I would run his household and my life in my own way, and he would not trouble me overmuch, just be happy to have a young wife while I spent his money on the things I desired."

"I am not a wealthy man, lady," Thomas said, "but I am not a poor one. I will give you a fine home to run, but I am afraid no one has ever called me malleable. I will have my way, though I cannot think of much I would deny you." He slid his fingers within her, just a slight amount, and she found a shiver of desire could rouse itself even in a sated body. "But I shall make sure you will not be uncompensated for my stubborn spirit."

He sobered. He took his hand from her and slid his arms beneath her, lifting her up in his arms in a smooth movement. He took them to the chair by the fire and sat down, with her cradled in his lap. "We must face Zorac, Lilith. Very soon, he will send his guards for us, if they are not already on their way."

Lilith swallowed. "My lord, what if—" she began to struggle away, to get to her feet, but he held her. "No, my lady. We will face him together."

"But what if he can undo,...I cannot bear to go back to being under the spell. If I do, you must do as I begged you. If you love me truly, you will release me, even if it means my death—"

"Hush," he whispered fiercely, grasping her hair in his hands and tugging it, hard. "Lilith, look at me. Look at me, now."

When she did, he gentled his touch. "You made a choice, lady, and I am here. We stand together."

He rose, lowering her to her feet, and went to his saddlebags. She could only watch his handsome, powerful torso in mute panic as he bent and withdrew a package from the bag. He unwrapped and shook out a gown of fine deep blue fabric, edged with a silver lace at the sleeve points, hem and modest neckline. There was a silk cotte of a sky blue color to go beneath it.

"For you, my lady. While you are beautiful in anything," he swept his glance over her, clothed in nothing but her hair and the firelight, "I will not have you displayed immodestly to others any longer."

Her fingers closed over the fabric, her panic settling into something much deeper and more painful as he gently pulled it from her touch, lifted it over her head. He threaded her arms through, helped slide the cotte down her body, adjusted it over her hips, his hand lingering on her waist. Then he helped her drape the silver edged gown over it.

She swallowed. "It is the first time, in a very long time, that I have not felt,...so naked." She lowered her head, and the sorrow on her face was hidden by the firelight and shadows. "You are too good to me, my lord."

"I could never be too good to you, my lady." From the same bag he withdrew a comb of polished wood, with carvings of leaves and flowers along the spine. He picked up a brush from the chair by the fire and began to brush out her long hair, freeing it from snarls with his fingers so he did not tug on her scalp. Apparently, grooming his stallion's long tail had made him adept at rendering his lady's equally long mane into warm silk that poured over his fingers.

"You would put a lady's maid to shame, sir," she said quietly, watching him in the mirror with eyes full of thoughts.

"You will never have a lady's maid with me," he said. "I will help dress you and fix your hair each morning, for you are my pleasure to care for."

"I find you just as pleasing to me, my lord," she offered shyly.

"It is good to hear, my lady."

They said nothing else. He finished her hair and drew it up from her face, fitting the comb against the crown of her head to hold it in place. He turned her to face him. Thomas's brow drew down as he looked at her. "What is it, Lilith?" he asked.

"I am not worthy of your love, my lord," she said.

Thomas's hands tightened on her shoulders.

"Why are you not worthy, lady? Is there a crime you have not paid for here? Do you believe you have not suffered enough to deserve your freedom from Zorac?"

A rueful smile touched her soft lips, lips she felt were swollen from his kisses. "I notice you do not offer me freedom from yourself, my lord."

Thomas did not smile. "In that, I am a selfish man, my lady, and you shall just have to get used to it. You must answer me, my lady, when I ask you a question."

"How much punishment is enough to pay for the taking of an innocent life?" she asked, her face full of pain.

A mailed fist struck the door, and she jumped beneath his hands before he could answer.

"My lord!" Cullen's voice was harsh. "Lord Zorac requires your presence, and that of the Lady Lilith, in the Great Hall. Immediately."

Chapter Five

Zorac was alone in the Hall. He bade Cullen and his guardsmen leave as soon as they brought Thomas and Lilith to him.

Thomas had donned his sword belt and dagger over his tunic. Cullen had not stopped him, had looked grimly amused. Thomas understood the message. Zorac had little to fear from weapons of steel.

The wizard sat now in his chair, watching them approach. His eyes were on Lilith. Thomas had made her place her hand on his, and so he escorted her as a knight would a lady, the gesture emphasizing that the spell was gone, and giving her cold fingers the warmth and reassurance of his own.

"So, my lord," Zorac's voice echoed in the empty hall. "You did it."

"No," Thomas shook his head. "Lady Lilith did it, my lord. She had the strength to win her own freedom. You know the tenets of this spell and you know it is so."

"Or perhaps Helene tricked me, and there was more to this spell. You think I am stupid, if you think I would believe that either of you has the power to overcome my magic. Seeing as you acted dishonorably, I am free to kill you both. Your victory is short-lived."

Lilith's eyes closed, her grip on Thomas's hand tightening. He felt her fear. It made Thomas furious.

"No," he stepped forward. "It is you who deceives, Zorac. You lie to yourself. Once, a long time ago, I saw a man go onto a battlefield, a man who represented all I believed was good and noble, who had all those qualities of the man I wished to be." His voice was hoarse with emotion, and he felt Lilith's hand on his arm. For the first time, he took comfort from his lady's touch. "When I next saw him, he was dead. I touched his body, pressed his blood to my lips, the last act of honor I could offer him then. I could have turned to hatred, but what would have happened if the disciples of Christ had done the same, my lord? What if they had chosen to turn their hands and minds to hate and destruction? You think you protect innocence, but are you not hoarding it here?"

He had the wizard's attention now, and perhaps his fury, but Thomas pressed on.

"My lady made a cruel choice as a child, and she has paid for her crime. The hardship you imposed on her brought forth this woman, a much different person from that selfish young girl. As in all quests that are part of God's purpose, she has changed and become far better than she was."

"Her face is the same," the wizard scoffed, surging to his feet. "The same treacherous face that compelled my brother to his death."

"Is it my face that so offends you, my lord?" Lilith said, taking Thomas by surprise with the raw anger in her voice. "Is it that which cannot allow you to forgive me, or yourself, for not being able to stop your brother from being as foolish as a cruel, ignorant girl? Here then, I shall help you."

In one swift stroke, she reached up, dug the nails of both of her hands into her left and right cheek, and tore ten stripes of flesh from beneath her eyes to her chin.

"My lady," Thomas was on her in an instant. He pulled her hands away from herself and pulled her back against his chest, his hands locking down on her wrists, crossing them against her body. "You will cease. Cease," he pressed his lips to her shaking temple.

As he tried to contain her efforts, he did not take his attention from Zorac, who was vibrating with a culmination of fury and emotion too great to be held within the walls of this room. The fire built and licked against the outer stones of the hearth, bathing them all in heat and the shadows of hellfire.

Lilith became still of a sudden. "Please let me go, my lord," she said softly.

"I will not."

"Please, Thomas." His name was a soft caress. "I will do myself no more harm, but I must be free to say what I wish to say to him."

Thomas looked down at her. She stared at Zorac and he at her, two wild, unpredictable animals gazing at each other over the expanse of a field, trying to determine who was prey and who was predator.

Thomas slowly released her wrists, but stayed where he was. She knelt, and spread the train of her skirt over his feet, her hips finding support against his calves, his body a bulwark behind her.

She made no attempt to wipe the blood from her face. Instead, she rubbed her palm over one cheek and extended her hand, smeared with her blood, toward the wizard.

"There is no stronger binding than blood in a spell," she said softly. "You told me this, when you seized my palm that day in my father's court and cut it with a knife to complete the spell you worked on me. It felt so strange. I, who had never felt the workings of the body in lust, suddenly felt so out of control, so animal-like. But I learned. Each humiliation you forced me to endure," her voice shook, "every rape of my mind and soul and body, I learned what it is to suffer. It was no great effort to figure out, in the end, that it was not your brother's suffering I was being forced to understand. It was yours. Your brother went to his death believing in the purity of love, believing his life was worth its sacrifice. He died in a peace you and I will likely never know."

Zorac snarled and turned his back on her, pacing to the fire. Thomas stood, tense behind her, trying to anticipate the man's actions, knowing he could likely incinerate them both without even looking at them.

"I know I will never ease your suffering, Lord Zorac. I know I will never make up for your loss. So if you must kill me, do so. That is now my choice. I simply pray you will do my lord no harm."

"No, my lady," Thomas snapped. "I forbid you to offer him your life."

"You call him 'my lord' now," Zorac said, his voice muffled by the fire.

"I do," she said. "I gave him that which you wished most from me, my heart and soul. He is my Master now, and you have no more claim on me, save that you may take my life."

Zorac stared at her. She stared back, but remained on her knees.

"What was my brother's name?" he asked, his voice faint, strange.

Lilith met his gaze without flinching. "I do not know, my lord. I forgot it, and you have never spoken his name to me, even when you brought me the necklace."

The wizard made an anguished roar, and his arm jerked out from his body as fast as the steel flashed from Thomas's scabbard. The knight leaped over her, and Lilith screamed his name.

The silver fire from the wizard crashed into the blade and wrapped around it, crackled down to the hand guard. The impact made Thomas stagger, took him to one knee, his profile still shielding his lady, knocking her with his shoulder so she tumbled back.

"Zorac, no!" she cried.

Thomas snarled and righted himself. The blade he held shimmered, a golden glow rising from the steel, rippling fingers of light that linked with the silver and bound the power of sun and moonlight together. He made it to his feet, still holding the sword upright. He met Zorac's hard gaze across twenty steps that separated life from death.

The golden light spread from the sword, over Thomas's hands, across his chest. The silver stayed firmly anchored to the blade. Zorac snarled, tried to loose his magic, but found it held fast in the golden grip.

Lilith scrambled to her knees, and the golden light washed over her, as if Thomas was becoming sunlight. She found herself surrounded by it, bathed in warmth. The short path to her lord had become a shifting, blinding path of diamonds, like the track the sun laid down upon the sea in the early mornings.

Come to me, my lady. His voice was in her head and she obeyed, pressing through that warmth until she was against the back of his calves. She curled her arms around his one leg, her fingers pressing into the hard muscle of his thigh, her cheek against the back of it.

Do not let him die. I can bear it all again, I truly can, but do not take him from me.

"Give way, my lord," Thomas said hoarsely. "Your vengeance is not worth this price to your soul. Give way, I say!"

With a snarl, Zorac loosed his hold on the barbed silver light and it crystallized and fell, shattering into pieces so there was a mirror of silver shards littering the golden pathway between him and Thomas.

The golden light became matter and slid over the silver, silver and gold embracing and becoming one. The light slid from Thomas's shoulders and cloaked Lilith entirely for a moment. The touch of such purity held simple forgiveness. She could forgive herself, and Zorac. She believed in the love Thomas offered her. She clung to his leg, weeping, until he lowered his sword and bent, lifting her gently to her feet, holding her close against his side with one arm.

The last of the light faded, but the floor was a mosaic of two colors that showed the path of power between the two men. A golden circle marked the floor around Thomas and Lilith, a silver disk around Zorac.

The wizard's face was haggard. "So you are a magician after all," he said.

Thomas shook his head, raised his sword arm to wipe at his face with the point of his wrist. "You know better than that, my lord. You could defeat me in time, for I do not control the power that comes to my defense."

"I could kill you," the wizard agreed. "But I would not defeat you."

Lilith cried out, seeing the blood on the hand Thomas had lowered to his side. Her hands sought his face, where blood ran from his nose and his right ear.

"Easy, lady, I am well," he bade her. "This Light, pure as its intentions are, is not always kind to poor mortal flesh."

"You will not let him hurt you," she insisted, her mouth

tight and stubborn. "I will not allow you to die for me."

"So you are giving the orders now, are you?" he teased her in a soft murmur, but he would not let her put her arms around him and hold him with her slim body covering the most vital parts of his. He set her to his side, and held her there, his sword point now to the ground, but not sheathed.

Zorac had not moved during this time, but now he did, sitting heavily in his chair and staring at the new design of his floor.

"My lord," Thomas said after the silence drew out long, and his lady's hand trembled on his arm. "I thank you for your hospitality, and ask your leave to depart, the lady Lilith with me."

Zorac's gaze rose. His eyes burned deep in his head as if he were fevered, or in great pain. "Does it matter whether I give you leave or not?" he croaked.

"It matters, my lord," Thomas's attention did not waver. "Not to me, but to you. You must let her go."

"Your powers let you do as you will."

"They are not mine, my lord. They come when they desire and I am not privy to the why. They felt this woman was worth defending. So did I. Perhaps they felt she had earned her release from your spell. Or perhaps the light was defending you."

At Zorac's startled look, Thomas inclined his head. "Much of what I see tells me you are a good man, Lord Zorac. Perhaps the light was keeping you from traveling down an even darker road than you have already."

Zorac's eyes closed. "Take her from here," he managed, his voice the growl of a wounded animal.

Thomas nodded, took his lady's arm, and guided her to the door.

"Let them go," Zorac snapped, when Cullen peered in around them. "And close the cursed door. I do not wish to be disturbed until...until I say so."

The guardsman gave a hesitant nod. Thomas and Lilith moved past him. When Cullen and one of his men shut the heavy double doors, a man in pain howled behind it.

§

Thomas kept Lilith with him, taking her back to the rooms to collect his things, delivering a short order on the way to Elias to prepare his horse. The word spread quickly through the castle, and none barred their way. The stable boy was waiting, the mount saddled, when they came back to the bailey, and he appreciated the boy's responsiveness. He did not desire to linger. Zorac's sound of pain had bordered on savage, and he knew wounded animals were unpredictable.

"Lady," the stable lad reached out, touched Lilith's waist. She knelt, and to the boy's surprise as much as Thomas's, she hugged him close. The little arms crept around her as he obviously warred between suitable manly behavior and the motherly attention an orphan craved from a sweet-smelling lady with gentle hands.

"You will take care of Lord Zorac," she said. "He will need your goodness, and Asneth's."

She held onto him tightly and he patted her hair, touched her cheeks. She laughed, and then she was crying, so Thomas knelt and held her when the boy squirmed away and ran.

She shook her head when at last she could speak. "It has been five years since I have been able to touch a boy child without the agony of the curse. As awful as it was to feel that way, I cannot express the horror of feeling that way when a *child* touched me, my lord. I tried to believe it was not the intent of his spell, that it was something he overlooked, that he would not have condoned such an abomination as that. Today, I believe that to be true. But oh, it feels good to hold a child again."

Thomas kissed her, a light caress, and lifted her up onto the horse, his hands staying at her waist. "Perhaps I shall give you a boy child all your own to hold, my lady. What think you of that? Zorac's spell prevented you from being fertile. It is so no longer."

She was stunned, and then she felt a becoming pink flush crept into her cheeks. "I would love to hold your child in my arms, my lord," her eyes darkened and she reached down, sliding back full into his arms, so he held her off the ground as she kissed him urgently, then tenderly, framing his face in her hands.

"I am afraid it is not real, my lord. That the dream will become the nightmare again."

"You can choose in dreams as well as life, my lady," he said, holding her as close and as tightly as he could without crushing her with his strength. "You have chosen, and this particular dream will have no more nightmares to it."

The stallion threw up his head and snorted as a bundle fell to the ground beside them. Thomas tensed and she looked up, where Zorac stood above them on the archway overlooking the courtyard, the same on which he had stood and faced outward to greet Thomas only a short day before.

"A gift to take with you," he said. His gaze flicked to Lilith and then back to Thomas. "To remember, for good or bad, that all choices have consequences."

She bent and picked up the bundle, a strand of the unicorn's mane exposed by the fall and the hasty wrapping.

"Lord Zorac."

The wizard had been turning away from them. At her voice, he stopped. Lilith waited, feeling Thomas's tension next to her. The wizard finally settled his gaze upon her, his body as still as a statue upon the wall of his castle.

"I spoke true, when I said I did not remember his name," Lilith said softly. "But when I came here, and found I had to create a soul, to give myself a place to go to survive each day, I found it was not born empty within me. It was a place filled with things I should have noticed. I remembered he was good, and kind in his ways, and you shared the same smile. I hope..." her voice faltered and Thomas put a supportive hand on her back.

She flinched, then relief swept across her face as she realized anew that the most casual touch would not arouse her to the painful lust. In time, she knew Thomas would teach her to do nothing but welcome his touch. It was a lesson she could look forward to learning.

"If you ever find it in your heart to do so, please know...I beg your forgiveness for taking him from you."

§

The horse had no fear of the unicorn's skin, but Lilith asked Thomas to carry it in the saddlebags, preferring to ride cloaked only by him. She sat before him on the horse, her body close, pressed in against his chest, her bottom between his legs, her legs over one of his thighs. He rode with her cradled thus in his arms, his cloak pulled around them both. He had not taken time to don his mail. He did not wish to tarry, he knew the people of Zorac's land were peaceful, and, most importantly, he wanted to feel her against his body.

She did not speak much, and Thomas did not disturb her. He watched her take in the world around her, seeing it through eyes no longer distracted by unabated need pouring through her body. Each bird's movement, each ray of the setting sun that flickered past an opening made by a fluttering leaf in the forest canopy, held her attention. At length, her body grew heavy and relaxed, and he pressed her jaw against her temple, comforting her as she slept, a deep easy rest.

He rode through the night, his horse not objecting since he set an easy pace, so as not to disturb his lady. His lady. The night was much like a dream itself, her softness in his arms, her sweet scent, the quiet of the forest, the routine of the creatures in it, unmolested by humans.

She was woken by the rays of the rising sun, and found herself still in his arms. They had stopped, standing on the edge of a clearing, where the meadow grass was as gold and rose as the sun rising above it.

"I dreamed of you, my lord," she breathed into his skin.

She felt his jaw move, and knew he smiled at the sound of her voice. She felt something move, deep within her. It was physical and emotional all at once. She tightened her hold around his waist and he responded in kind, surrounding her with his strength and warmth.

"And was the dream pleasurable, my lady?"

"Almost as pleasurable as waking up in your arms, my lord. I've no other desire beyond that, ever again, I think."

Thomas tipped her chin back and drank from her lips. They trembled beneath his and he deepened the kiss, until her hands were gripping his shirt in two fists.

His hand gently touched her cheek, where she had scored herself.

"You should not have done this," he murmured. "You must never hurt yourself, it displeases me greatly."

"And what of you?" she looked up, touched her hand to his ear, where the blood had dried to a brittle crimson crust yet to be sponged away by her cozening. "It displeases me to see you harmed, as well."

"You will take good care of me, I am sure, my lady, and be sure I do not displease you often."

"I am at a loss, my lord," she said softly. "It will be some time before I know my place in the world. I may be a poor mistress in your home."

"You are the only mistress for my home, and your place will always be with me," he asserted. "If you will still have me."

At her surprised look, he lifted a shoulder. "I told you, my lady, accepting me as your lord and Master is your choice, and it always will be. Though be fair warned," he gave her a look that tightened things low in her stomach and brought a flush to her cheeks, "I will never make it easy for you to choose otherwise."

His lips were upon hers again, and the kiss went from spiritual to ravenous in no more than a breath, leaving her gasping in his arms. He raised his head, cursing himself for the need for restraint, but his lady took care of his worries.

"Take me here, my lord, under the first light of this new day. I want to feel you within me, as it was in my dream. I want the stroke of your lance to burn away the touch of all others and leave me branded by you only."

"It is perhaps too soon, lady. I can certainly contain my desire and give you time."

"My lord," she looked up at him, those dark eyes alive with need, and a promise of the smile he knew he would coax from her when her heart had healed under his care. "I am asking my Master to fulfill my desires. Will he deny me? I need you, my lord," she added quietly. "What I experienced in Zorac's castle is no more like what I share with you than taking the sacrament is to spitting in the dirt. I feel I have been empty so long, I need you to fill my body to fill my heart. Please do not make me beg."

"Forgive me, lady," he swung down, a smile in his voice. He took her with him, carrying her in his arms. "I forgot. As your Master, my first task is always to serve your desires."

"Yes, my lord."

The End

Threads of Faith

A Paranormal Erotic Romance Novella

Joey W. Hill

Chapter One

"I know you're there," the old woman murmured. She inched forward on her knees and pulled a handful of weeds from the tangle at the base of the rose bushes. The heavy clusters of blooms arched over her head, tickling her nape with their silk petals and her nose with their heavy fragrance.

"Ow!" She laughed and made a grab at the black paw that shot out from the cover of the hedge to bat at her hand. The claws had been sheathed. It was her instinctive jerk that caused her pain, knocking her hand into the thorns.

"Beezle, you are a menace. One of these days I'm going to have cat stew for dinner."

A whisper of breeze, a rustle, and she realized she had let down her guard. She spun around, a hand up, and the stone struck her forehead, propelling her frail body back into the bushes, thorns pricking through her light cotton dress like a bed of nails. She heard Beezle scramble away, frightened. She was frightened too because her head was spinning and she couldn't marshal her wits to raise a defense.

The laughter of teenagers was reassuring, their act of unkindness likely a fleeting gesture of bored cruelty as they pressed on to mischief deeper into the woods.

She was wrong. Another stone struck the bridge of her nose and she cried out, averting her face. The pain drove her to one knee.

"Ain't no one around to help you, you old witch." The jeer came from the trees. "You're all alone, and we're gonna get you!"

Cackling laughter. She struggled to right herself. If she could just focus, get her sense of balance together...

"Jesus fucking Christ!" A frightened yelp and a crash, as if someone had been tossed out of a tree. Was that a snarl?

Marisa staggered toward her door and stumbled over her garden tools. The world was blurry, and something warm and wet trickled down her forehead into her left eye and mouth. Metal and salt, substance of earth, of herself.

"Wards of earth, fire, water and wind, may your powers rise and blend. Take this home out of evil's view, Lord and Lady allow no harm to break through," she rasped, seeking to connect to the power. The concussion made the connection tenuous, and the wards flickered weakly, even where she could discern them on the clearing's edge. Fear clutched her low in her stomach. She'd not been this vulnerable in a long time.

A pair of feet came toward her. She crawled across the ground and clasped a rock, perhaps the same rock that had struck her. She could see the fragility of her blue-veined hand, the skin shimmering beneath her gaze. No, surely she was not that weak. The illusion spell had a life of its own. She had made sure it existed separate from her consciousness.

The feet, sizeable ones in hiking boots, were attached to long calves and a pair of muscular thighs. Her attacker had the physique of a lineman for the school football team. She tried to scramble away, but he caught her in one stride.

She squalled like Beezle and turned on him, the rock gripped in her fist. Even wounded, she was quick, but he was more so, and caught her wrist in a strong grip.

"Be easy, miss. They're gone. I ran them off. It's all right."

His voice stroked her frantic emotions, soothed them down, even as his hands gentled her physically. She felt his fingers stroke her hair. Not the brittle and sparse strands of an aging woman but the raven, waist-length locks of her true form.

"No," she whispered. The only thing that could dissolve the spell was a more powerful witch, or a person who possessed True Sight.

"It's all right," he repeated, and gathered her to him. He lifted her off the ground easily, as if she were a child, and gave her the words of universal comfort, as empty as they might be. "I won't let anything happen to you."

Her heavy head wobbled onto his shoulder. His fingers tangled in her hair at her shoulder, his other hand curled around her thigh beneath her plain calico smock dress.

Men did not touch her. Most women did not. It was shocking, this easy familiarity of a man's hands upon her. People were afraid to touch a witch, even if they claimed not to believe she was one. They stood at her door with averted eyes and insisted they were there on a dare or a lark. The way he held her was possessive, intimate, as if they knew one another far better than they did.

He stepped across the open threshold to her three-room home. "Where's your bed, miss?"

She shook her head. "Just put me down in the kitchen chair," she said. "Sitting up will help me get my wits about me."

"If you had your wits about you, you wouldn't be living out here in the middle of nowhere with no one to protect you."

She aimed a frosty glare at him and collided with a sexual heat that startled her. It threatened to melt her ire before it could be vented.

He had eyes like Beezle's, a yellow-green, but more blended, a vibrant hazel. His hair was the brown of rich, dark earth, almost black. Brows like slivers of fine dark silk and firm lips that looked somewhat angry at the moment, but once she saw him clearly, she wasn't afraid. His face had the strength of character immortalized by old film. Jimmy Stewart, Gary Cooper, Gregory Peck. The face of a white knight, a hero, the man who would never think to leave women and children behind, who would guard the back of a friend no matter the cost, who would face up to his mistakes with the same unflinching courage. He possessed the True Sight. To her trained gaze, it was as obvious as the fact he was a man. He would see through any spell, any deception, the smallest white lie.

He wore a brown soft twill shirt and blue jeans. Not tight, but snug in the way that men of good physique wore them. He smelled like sweat and soap and a light aftershave.

"My name is Conlon," he said with a nod. "Conlon Maguire."

"Marisa," she responded automatically. "I'm fine now. I appreciate your kindness, but I don't need—"

"I was coming to see you."

"Oh." That startled her into silence. People only came to her door for one reason, and she found that reason hard to reconcile with the handsome, confident man standing in her kitchen.

He found a cloth in her sink, a basin of water she drew from the deep creek behind her home. "Here." He touched at the blood on the bridge of her nose, catching her chin to hold her still. He ignored the hand she latched onto his powerful wrist to tug his touch away.

"I can do it."

"I'm sure you can but I want to do it, so be still, kitten, and stop squirming."

His shirt was open at the neck so the fabric gapped with the forward cant of his body. She saw the smooth curve of a pectoral and a soft pelt of chest hair, narrowing down to a line over a flat, muscular stomach. After that it was shadows, as the shirt tucked into his waistband. She pulled her gaze away, back to his face, which was intent on hers, washing away the blood with small gentle pressures on her forehead, her nose, her lips. He cradled the side of her face as he moved downward. What would it be like to feel his fingers delve into her hair, tug her head back so that he could place those firm lips over hers?

The unexpected thought surprised her. Men did not interest her. This was her quiet world, the world she had created for herself with great effort and painful sacrifice. Her wits were just beyond her fingertips, waiting for her to reach out and reclaim control of them and the situation.

He pushed back the hair over her left ear and the damp cloth slid there, touching in those tiny crevices. The trickle of blood and dirt down her neck went next as he moved his touch there. His thumb rubbed her jugular, his fingers curved around the side of her throat. Her wits moved a deliberate step out of reach as she discovered how sensitive her throat was to a man's caress.

Her cats rubbed against her in affection and slept close to her at night for companionship, but this man's hands made her think of wild, unsettling actions, far beyond affection. With little effort, she could imagine his body heat and strength curled around her as well as her cats, keeping them all safe while they dreamed.

Marisa surged out of the chair and clambered over his knee awkwardly to get into the more open space of the kitchen. He rose and the kitchen shrank.

"How...how did you get here?"

"They told me it wasn't accessible by car so I hiked in. I thought it odd, an elderly woman living so far from civilization. They didn't mention you." His gaze coursed down her body in a way that flustered her.

"You're teasing me, sir," she said coolly. "You and I both know you can see through the illusion I maintain. Further, I doubt someone who looks like you needs a potion to attract a woman. So perhaps you should tell me why you are really here."

He reached out, and the table behind her blocked her retreat. He caught his fingers in her hair, wrapped it once around his knuckles so she was tethered to him. He pulled her a step toward him.

"Based upon the illusion you maintain, Marisa, I'd say you already know that looks don't bring you everything you desire. Sometimes it brings things you don't want at all."

Like big, unsettling men in her kitchen. His body and hers were only a deep breath apart, and she felt their auras touching, exploring the shape of one another. Her fingers were itching to do the same, to tug his shirt from his waistband, feel the hard line of those muscles. She wanted to let her fingers glide through the soft hairs on his stomach and chest and get to know the hot skin and muscle beneath.

Despite the table, she did take a step back, and the legs scraped their complaint on the wood floor. There was a strange feeling in her chest, and it was moving lower. It grew more noticeable each time she drew in his scent and met those steady, hazel eyes.

Potion. He was here for a potion. What was the matter with her? Perhaps that rock had done her genuine harm. Perhaps she should consider a trip into town to the doctor.

"Even if I weren't here for a potion," he added, "you're stuck with me for awhile. I'm not leaving until I'm sure you're okay."

"You can't stay on my property if I tell you to leave," she said. "That's trespassing."

"Call a cop," he responded. "Oh, that's right. No phone." He glanced around. "No electricity." His fingers curled around the back of her neck, and she snapped her glance up to him, uneasy. "No way to call for help if you were injured or needed help."

"You seem overly obsessed with my protection, Mr. Maguire," she managed. "If it makes you feel better, I have a two-way radio for emergencies, and I keep transportation in my shed if I need it."

"A broom?"

She narrowed her eyes and jerked free. "I'm beginning to see why you need a potion."

When he smiled, she saw a dimple at the left corner of his mouth. "So you think you can help me then?"

"The potion makes that decision. I just mix it. Belief is important to its success. If you're here as a joke or on a dare, then the potion will be useless to you."

"What's the cost?"

"The potion also sets the price. The magic that fuels it speaks to me and tells me what it demands in exchange."

"That's convenient."

"That's how I acquired my mansion and Ferrari, Mr. Maguire," she said dryly, circling around the table to her cabinets. "It usually requires acts of service," she added, "not donations to me. I am bound by its will as much as the recipient. The seed of love must be there, and the person must be willing in their hearts to accept the potion's will. You can have a seat if you like. This will take a few minutes."

"Can I get things together for you?" He frowned, studying her unsteady movements, the cut on her head. "I told you I'm not leaving until I'm sure you're all right. You can take your time."

"I'm fine, really. I'm getting my bearings back."

The sooner she made what he wanted and assured him of her health, the sooner he would go, him and his disturbing presence. So she opened the doors of the large oak cabinet on the wall, revealing a larder full of bottles and jars with a rainbow of liquid and plant contents.

"I need to focus for a few moments in silence," she said, her back to him.

"All right," he murmured, and the tone of his voice told her he was watching her with a penetrating intensity that sank into her skin and bones like the warmth of the sun. She drew a deep breath. Despite her personal preferences, she did not block him. No matter Conlon Maguire's arrogance, at the moment he was part of the Web that bound them all, the body of the Lord and Lady, one of the many cells of the blood that ran through Their Veins. She accepted his presence, his life force, into the circle of her own. She let the magic feel his shape and form, his worthiness, purpose and desires.

The exercise always gave her a necessary sense of a person. Usually it was a fleeting touch, like the brushed kiss of acquaintances. In this instance, the soul of Conlon Maguire reached out and surrounded hers and pulled her into him. She felt the man from the inside out.

He was a man of True Sight, as she had already sensed. A man who would always protect those weaker than himself. A man generous in opening his heart but who had never given his heart away to a woman. A man who liked to laugh, a physical man, a man who would not be denied what he wanted. Heat washed through her, and for a moment she was in the body of the woman he sought. His chest pressed against the softness of her breasts. His hands clasped her waist, his palms sliding down to cup the cheeks of her backside, holding her against his rigid desire. She felt it move against the quickening flesh between her thighs. His tongue claimed hers. The name of the woman hovered on his lips. Marisa struggled to hear that name, though she had never before asked or tried to discover the name of a person for whom a potion was mixed.

She started out of the vision, her pulse pounding.

"Are you all right?"

Marisa nodded, a quick jerk, and held up her finger to keep him back. "The magic has agreed to mix a potion for you."

With unsteady hands, she withdrew three of the four ingredients she would need and set them on the sideboard.

The potion didn't often call for the fourth ingredient, and so she turned to drag her chair over to use it as a stepping stool. She bumped into him. He stood behind her, considering all her bottles and jars. Conlon looked down at her. "Which one, kitten?"

She frowned and pointed. He reached up and over her and took down the large jar with one hand, putting it into both of her waiting ones.

Something curled in her stomach, unsettling but not unpleasant, roused by the unfamiliar sensation of being able to count on someone's help, someone's strengths balancing out her needs.

She nodded courteously and skirted around him, going to where the other ingredients waited. She spread out a clean linen cloth and laid the herbs she had chosen on it. Marisa took up her athame, a curved and sharp blade of stainless steel she had fired and stamped herself, and cut the proper measure. She dropped the plants into a mortar and pestle carved of white stone.

He had turned from his study of her stores to a study of her, and she felt a need to fill the silence that seemed too comfortable to be having with a stranger.

"So why will this woman not have you?"

While she did not ask names, she did sometimes ask other things to help the potion along by giving the seeker an additional dose of common sense. In this case, she suspected her motives were not quite so selfless.

"I think she will, but she's very unique. I need a special approach, something to help me get my foot in the door."

Marisa nodded. She ground the herbs with deliberate

turns of the pestle, infusing them with the power of the Lord and Lady and of the four elements. When she was satisfied, she scooped the herbs out and dropped them into the small cauldron of water she had simmering on a gas burner. Curious, she dipped a spoon into it to get a sense of what color the steeped mixture would take.

This time it was going to be Marisa's favorite, a sparkling amethyst, but the sight of the hue startled her. Amethyst was the color of strongest intent. This man's request was closely aligned with the Lord and Lady's Will, and great good would emanate along the strands of the Web from its success. It was almost a certainty that, with or without the potion, his suit for his chosen lady would prevail.

Why should she be surprised? Only those of pure hearts, coupled with great courage and integrity, were blessed with the True Sight. Perhaps that was one of the reasons she felt so disturbed around him. There was nothing she could hide from him, and yet he was not a man from whom one *needed* to hide.

She took the small cauldron from the burner and set it on a quilted square potholder on the sideboard. The linen cloth went over the top to protect it from debris in the air while it steeped and to block the steam from scorching her face as she leaned over it. Marisa placed her palms flat on either side of the cauldron, cleared her mind, opened her energy centers and drew in the aroma, waiting for the magic to tell her the price of the potion.

The answer was immediate, a rush of information and images that were clear and impossible to misunderstand. Regardless, Marisa asked again. The same answer came, just as clearly. Emphatically.

She took her hands away and stepped back. She was a servant of the Craft, a priestess, and she was obedient to the Will of the Light. She understood that Its ways might be beyond her understanding, but that they were what was meant to be. This was the first time she had ever thought the Lord and Lady might have fried a circuit.

"Problem?"

Conlon had taken a seat on the other side of the table to

watch her finish the preparations, and now her desperate eyes flitted to him. He should have looked out of place in her kitchen, but he didn't. In fact, she could well imagine him being there every day, watching her with those intent hazel eyes that became gilded verdigris in the shadowed light inside her home.

She continued to stare at him, speechless, her face drained of color. Frowning, he rose and came around the table. It drew her attention to the broadness of his shoulders, the lean strength of his thighs, the fine structure and power of the man beneath the clothes. He reached forward as if to lift the cloth and see what had caused her such consternation.

"Don't." The word snapped out of her like a whip. "You can't touch it until you hear its cost."

"All right." He settled back, his hips propped against her table. He crossed his arms across his chest and hooked his fingers under his armpits. She was distracted by the firm, unsmiling curve of his lips. For some reason, she wanted to reach out, trace them with her fingertips, feel their texture.

"Tell me," he prompted, lifting a brow at her startled jerk.

Just say it, and it will be over. He can refuse, and it will be nothing to you.

That was a lie and she knew it. The color of this potion said his intent would serve the highest good. The love he pursued, if consummated and brought to be, would enhance the Pattern and the Will of the Lord and Lady. How could she refuse? How could she possibly find the courage to convince him if *he* refused?

"You must lie with me by full moonrise tonight. That is the potion's price."

Surprise crossed his features, but not the pigment-draining shock she had experienced. He straightened, freeing his arms, drawing her eye to the way his fingers slid across his own skin. "You are sure."

"The voice is clear enough." She rubbed her temple. "You know I do not lie. You have the right to refuse, and the potion becomes powerless. The Lord and Lady's Will is focused through the potion, but it is a tool. You may find your desires will prevail without it if They support your cause."

There, that was fair. Hadn't she thought much the same thing when she first explored his soul? "If you believe in honesty, the woman you desire may be displeased with the price you paid to win her heart, regardless," she added, a bit tartly.

Conlon gave her an even look and stepped forward. Marisa did not move, her body frozen like an anxious doe. Her head tilted back as he got closer so she could still meet his gaze. She had her hand over the linen cloth and could feel the heat of the cauldron's lip beneath it. He laid his hand over hers, covering her fingers and bringing his own in shared contact with the potion's vessel.

"What about you, Marisa?" He reached out, touched her chin with a fingertip. "You don't have to accept the potion's price. I want the love of this woman, but I won't have it at the price of forcing your affections."

While his words did not ease the quaking in her belly, it reminded her that he was an honorable man. An honorable man deserved a truthful response.

"I serve the Light, Conlon, and if it says this is the price of your potion, and the love you seek serves Their Will, then I will obey it. I know it serves a greater purpose than my own fears."

"Fears?" His brow furrowed, and his touch became a firm hold on her delicate jaw. "Tell me what you fear."

"I just..." She couldn't avert her face, but she did shift her gaze to the wall, feeling heat wash over her skin under his fingertips. "I've never done this, Conlon." She crossed her arms over her body, a protective gesture she knew suggested vulnerability, but she could not stop herself from making the gesture of self-comfort. "I'll be fine," she said more firmly. "I just need a little time to get used to the idea."

He studied her, and his hand gentled, stroking her cheek, so she looked at him. "You *will* be fine. I won't hurt you, Marisa. I'll make sure you feel only pleasure, no pain."

His easy acquiescence startled her. "Are you sure? What of this woman? Won't she..."

"The people in town hold your power and your potions in very high regard, Marisa. You've told me my cause is true, and that the potion has named a price. I want this woman for my own."

She nodded, a quick dip of her head. "Then you must say you accept the potion's price, out loud." She put her hand back on the cauldron, over his this time. The firm skin, the light layer of hair on his knuckles, felt different to her, intriguing.

"I accept this potion's price," he said formally, his gaze never leaving hers, "because the woman I wish to claim is the total of my desires. I knew the moment I heard her name that she is mine. I knew when I first saw her that she is the one. The only."

He was wrong. He would cause her pain, a shrieking banshee within the hollow emptiness of her chest. To have someone want her like he wanted, that was beyond anything Marisa could hope for in her reality. From the time she was born, isolation had been required for her survival. Now she must bear to have such a man in her arms for nearly a full day, knowing he was only there for another, and let it shatter her, as she knew it must.

She slid her hand off his. "The potion is now charged. When you leave me, I will put it in a flask, and you will share it with this woman, and the Lord and Lady's Will be done." She found her palms nervously damp and wiped them on her skirt.

"Marisa," Conlon bent his knees to catch her eye, a reassuring look on his face. He took her hands in both of his. "I assume the potion doesn't require us to hop on each other like rabbits. We can take some time to get to know each other. Enjoy each other. The sun's still high in the sky."

Enjoy a taste of something she might never have again. But every day was like that, wasn't it? Today might be the last day she got to watch dew melt off a flower or see Beezle chase a butterfly across the yard. If today was all she had, how could she spend any part of it regretting what she might not have tomorrow?

She took a deep breath, nodded her head.

Quirking his brow to give her some warning, Conlon exerted a gradual but inexorable pressure on their linked fingers, bringing her closer to him until she leaned into his body. He folded one of her palms low on his waist, over his hipbone. She felt his warmth, the softness of the shirt, and the firmness of him under her touch.

"Your willingness is a precious gift to me," he said. His voice dropped, got rougher in a way she liked, though she didn't know why. "Every man hopes to be a woman's first lover, to experience her innocence."

"To take it."

"To open and pleasure it, together." His face drew closer to her upturned one, and his arm slid around her waist, gathering her up against him.

He did not let her other hand go when he brought her to him. As his arm came behind her, he took her hand with it, turning her wrist so her elbow bent and her arm folded up behind her back. The position pushed her breasts up and forward, displaying them on the hard platform of his chest. He increased the pressure and pushed her up onto her toes, his fingers laced through hers at the small of her back. The ends of his fingers curled into the skirt and dug into the thin elastic band beneath, so she felt a tug on her panties against the sensitive cheeks of her bottom.

"I'm afraid," was all she managed. His lips touched hers at the moment she formed the words, so his tongue eased between her parted lips, and his mouth closed over hers, sealing in the heat.

She had been kissed once years ago by a boy who had been dared to kiss her. That swipe of clammy lips was so far from Conlon's kiss that she forever discarded the idea of even calling it a kiss.

Surely the bones had melted in her body because all of a sudden she couldn't stand on her own. She lifted her hand from his hip and gripped his shirt at his ribs for balance. He caught the back of her head in his large palm, his fingers in her hair, and deepened the thrust of his tongue. He ran it along the edges of her teeth, the inside of her cheek, learning her, and stroked the quivering surface of her tongue with his when he was done with that.

His body was all a new experience to her, the hard muscle, the musk of sweat from hiking through the woods, male. No doubt of the last, as the strength of his hold against the small of her back pressed her against a hard ridge growing larger under straining denim. It rubbed against her belly, and her hips rocked forward in an instinctive reaction to it. The place between her legs contracted with a startling sensation that flooded her body.

A key turned, tumbling open a locked room of her subconscious. It was as if she was a person who had wandered in a desert for so long that she did not know she was thirsty until someone offered her a glass of ice water. Her thirst was abrupt, all-consuming, but she found herself staring at that glass, lacking the knowledge of how to reach out and bring it to her lips.

It was disturbing to have to depend on him. She was helpless to do anything but let him lead. Academically, Marisa knew the urges of the human body, but she had divorced herself from her own. With one kiss, he was reconciling her with them.

His middle finger straightened and pressed against the thin gauze fabric of her skirt, even as his other fingers remained intertwined with hers at her lower back. He insinuated the fabric of the skirt, along with his finger, under the waistband of her panties and rubbed a small vertical stroke in the dip at the top of her buttocks. Marisa gasped into his mouth. She wiggled against the touch, against his strength, increasing the friction. He tightened his grip and her feet left the floor. He settled the apex of her thighs directly over that hard ridge in his jeans. She moaned at the pressure and panic filtered in as she floundered in the wash of unfamiliar sensations.

"Stop," she managed against his mouth. "Please, let go...let me down." She turned her head so her cheek was pressed hard against his jaw, hiding her face. His fingers stilled and she felt his unsteady breaths moving the loosened strands of her hair against her skin. Slowly the grasp of his fingers in her scalp eased off and became a caressing stroke. His chest expanded beneath her breasts, a slow, deep breath, and he let her down, one inch at a time.

She had to bite her lip as that hard part of him dragged along her vibrating tissues.

He did not let her feet touch the ground. As she slid down those excruciating inches, his thigh came forward, parting her legs. She came to a halt seated on that column of muscle that shifted against her throbbing center.

"Holy Mother, you could make a man lose his mind with one kiss, Marisa. No wonder they call you a witch."

"I suspect that's not the reason," she whispered. His eyes were now pure gold because heat had melted the green, like the summer sun burnishing everything in a meadow. His lips were moist from her mouth.

He held her fast as she made to wriggle free. "No, Marisa. If we're going to do this, I want you to be thinking about having me there, and keeping your mind on it. Do you know what this is?" He lifted his ankle, so he increased the pressure of his thigh between her legs.

"Of course." She tried to be casual but knew her flushed wild expression and trembling body betrayed her. "I'm a virgin, Conlon, not ignorant."

"Tell me, then."

"It is..." She blew out a breath, shot him a glare that seemed to amuse him, "it's my vagina."

He smiled, passed a thumb over her lip. "You said that so primly, like my sex ed teacher Mrs. Patterson."

"You never needed a sexual education teacher," she retorted. "Etiquette class wouldn't have been amiss, however."

"You also speak like you've spent more time reading than talking," he observed. "All formal. 'Amiss'. I haven't heard that word used in years." He increased his hold on the hand he still held pinned at the small of her back and began to rock his foot, heel to toe, counterbalancing it with the strength of his arm so he was rocking her back and forth on his long leg.

"How about this, Teacher?" His teeth nipped at her ear. "Pussy. Cunt. I like both of those. Cunt reminds me of a cave, deep underground, with a hot spring. The steam condensing and glistening on the slick inner walls, creating a smell of heat and earth, the way your cunt would smell if

I buried my nose in it. Or pussy, like a pussy willow, soft under my fingertips, but round and firm too, the size of a finger pad, like your clit is." With a ripple of muscle, he stroked her in that exact spot, so no further English lesson was needed to identify it for her.

"I said I needed to go slow," she said desperately, clutching at his shoulder for balance as he worked his leg against her pussy.

"I plan to, Marisa. I won't try to claim your maidenhead until nightfall, and it's barely lunchtime now. I want you wet and aroused so you won't be afraid."

"It's...you're making it hard for me to think," she said.

He smiled, though there was a tension around his mouth, and his eyes were a fire of desire that was almost as effective on her senses as his leg's movement. He began to bounce his leg gently. Since he kept her seated hard against him with that one relentless hand, each impact sent a ripple to her womb. Her breasts moved freely beneath the loose smock and his eyes followed their quivering movement.

"I...I need to know more about you," she managed, trying to fight off the spiral of sensations that screamed from that jarring focal point between her legs.

He let her go abruptly and caught both hands in her hair. She fell against him but froze at the ferocious need in his face. His mouth hovered just above hers, touching her with the heat of his breath as he spoke. "No man has ever had you, truly?"

"You know I speak the truth," she said, her body trembling against his.

"Yes," he said. "But your body responds like a woman born for sensual pleasure."

She pushed away, shaking her head, and he took her hand, holding it in a secure grip. She moved as far back as that link would allow and tried to keep her attention on his face rather than the heat and need vibrating off that powerful body.

"Please, Conlon, I can't. This feels too fast. My body understands your desires and appears all too willing to capitulate, but I have to face myself in the mirror when you're gone. Whether it be the Lord and Lady's Will or no, I need to get my balance."

"All right." In a gesture that surprised her with its tenderness, he raised both her hands, brushed his lips across her knuckles. "So how do you want to do this?"

She pushed her hair off her forehead, a confused scrubbing motion. "What do you do for a living?"

He smiled, and something in her stomach tilted like the corners of his mouth. "Security. Professional bodyguard."

She blinked. "Like Secret Service?"

"Not anymore. I do private jobs. Businessmen traveling in countries with unstable governments, celebrities being stalked, witness protection work occasionally."

A protector, a white knight. Her initial vision had been more accurate than she expected.

"So you don't have much time to develop a relationship. The potion's a way to sidestep all that."

"Now see, that's why I didn't want to ease off," he said, tightening his grip on her fingers. "You want to retreat behind that serpent tongue of yours. It's a lot sweeter when it's occupied with something, like mine."

"I want to take a swim in the creek and get cleaned up." She backed away, keeping the tether of their arms taut. "I've been gardening all morning. I'm sweaty and dirty, and I've got blood drying in my hair."

"So you do." His gaze went back to the spot, and he released one hand to touch her there, gently on the sore area, though the slightest pressure made her wince. "Okay, let's go do that."

"What? I meant—" Marisa had to swallow the rest of the statement because he was guiding her out the door. He stepped neatly over Beezle, now stretched across the sun-drenched threshold. The black cat seemed utterly unconcerned by the big man's presence in their home. Marisa tripped over him, and the cat gave her an aggrieved look.

"As familiars go, he's not tremendously intimidating," Conlon observed, dragging her along with him around the corner of the house, headed for the creek where she did her washing. He paused, glanced down at her. "There's not much to screen you here from Peeping Toms."

"I don't get many visitors, and those I do see an old woman. They're not interested in watching an eighty-year-old crone bathe."

"Maybe because they're looking at the flesh, not the woman. You'd be beautiful at any age, Marisa."

What was it about that steady gaze and set mouth that made her believe him? It raised that pain in her heart again, that futile wish for someone who would say such words to her, for her. Someone who wouldn't be afraid of her, who would be willing to stand by her as the inevitable changes of time altered her body but not her mind. Not her need to be loved and cherished, not the need to be thought beautiful and worthy of love.

Such a person would be a quiet man. Perhaps a bookish sort with wire-rimmed glasses that liked to garden, like her. Certainly not a large, overbearing brute of a man with gentle, powerful hands and a mouth that turned her brain into a bowl of soup.

"How about I sit here while you bathe? Do you need a towel, soap?" At her look, he raised a shoulder. "If we've both accepted the potion's terms, I'm going to see you unclothed eventually. Wouldn't it be easier to get used to it, in a way like this, where you've got some distance from me?"

"Do you always take over?" she demanded.

He slid his hands into the back pockets of his jeans and cocked a hip, studying her. The posture only enhanced the size of his chest, the pull of the cloth against the impressive pectorals. "You said you wanted to take a bath," he pointed out, as if that were a reasonable response to her question rather than an absolutely irrelevant point.

She turned her back on him to face the waters of the creek. The midday song of the cicadas vibrated patterns against the heavy summer air. She heard the far-off call of a hawk and smelled the mint in her nearby herb garden.

Conlon let her be a moment as she watched the current move. The shallows gurgled over slick rocks and dampened the sand on the banks. The deeper waters in the center moved in a tranquil but inexorable progress toward their destination, the Broken Sound River, a hundred miles to the south, which would eventually pour into the Atlantic.

Is this what she wanted? The potion had set the price, and she had never questioned it, but Conlon had asked her what *she* wanted. He had given her the choice. She was just scared. She had not been this close to another person, had not spent this much time with one, in a long time. Marisa now knew how to keep herself from shattering and letting in the images that could destroy her mind, as they had come close to doing too many times. Intimacy had the power to undermine her efforts, strip down her shields. Conlon already could see through her illusion magic. Could she protect herself and honor the potion?

She steadied herself with a mental shake. She had to trust the Lord and Lady knew what They were doing. She would have to trust Conlon.

As if he knew the conclusion she had reached, he moved. She heard him approach her, his hiking shoes moving deliberately over the ground. His hands, large and capable, settled on her shoulders and rested there a moment. He gathered her hair in one hand, pushed it over her left shoulder, revealing her nape and the fragile joining of her right shoulder to her neck.

She watched the water and trembled as his fingers unhooked the row of buttons down the back. The dress was loose and could easily lift over her head, but she did not stop him from working each button through its eyelet, his knuckles brushing the bumps of her spine and the shallow channel of it as he worked his way to her waist. He pushed the sleeves down her unresisting arms so the bodice tumbled to her waist and pooled low on the flare of her hips, one button away from dropping the dress to her ankles.

The warm summer air and his breath mixed, touching her bare shoulder, and then his lips were there, tasting her flesh at that sensitive juncture. She had her head bowed, so she watched gooseflesh prickle up along the tops of her breasts. The shape and color of her nipples shifted from a soft pale pink, like impatiens growing in the shade provided by an oak's canopy, to a deep, sun-kissed mauve bud.

She stayed very, very still. Being touched at all, let alone being touched like this, was new to her, and she wasn't sure if there was a right way to react. His lips felt good on her neck. They felt wonderful there.

His light kiss turned into a nibble, and her nipples grew fuller and longer, like stamens attracting the ministrations of the plush-backed bumblebee. Only in this case, the flower's response to heat attracted the stroke of Conlon's fingers. She tensed as his hands cupped her breasts, and the thumbs rubbed over the tips. She shuddered, her bare shoulder blades making contact with his shirt front, her bottom brushing the crotch of his jeans and tops of his thighs, causing those fingers to tighten.

"A further lesson in vocabulary, Teacher," he said against her ear. "These," his hands lifted her breasts, brought them together before her eyes with the reverence of an offering to the gods, "are the most beautiful tits I've ever seen. When I see your nipples tight like this, I want to suck on them until you come, just from the pull of my mouth."

His palms slid down to the curve of her hips, leaving her breasts aching. She felt the lingering imprint of his hands as if they were still there. With a flick, another button was free. The garment fell to her ankles, leaving her standing in her panties. His thumbs hooked in their elastic and slid them down her thighs. She had to turn and place a hand on his shoulder to balance herself as she stepped out of them. He rolled them into a neat ball and folded them up in her dress, laying them to the side. His hand at her hip held her to his side as he straightened. She stared down at her left bare breast, raised up higher than the right by the pressure of his body against it.

"Now," his voice was husky above her ear, his jawline brushing the crown of her head. "Go wash for me. I want to watch you."

Marisa swallowed. Took one step then another away from the shelter and imposition of his body. She focused on the creek, its laughing banks, its somber and thoughtful depths.

She kept a covered basket near the edge and she bent, her long hair falling forward and brushing her knees as she retrieved the soap and cloth there. His indrawn breath drew her gaze back to him. He stood stock still, his gaze coursing over her heart-shaped bottom and what her bent position revealed to him. She straightened quickly, flushing, and stepped into the water, the familiar warm mud sucking at her toes. Minnows brushed her calves as they scampered out of her path.

The water rose to her hips and then her waist. It was above her head from here, so she dropped below the surface to wet her hair. She swam a few strokes and rolled over beneath the water's surface, feeling in wonder the different texture of the water on her heated, aroused skin.

She knew about sex the way she knew how to mix vinegar and water to make a universal cleaner. She did not create the elements, did not truly understand how bringing them together achieved such a simple but effective purpose, but she knew how to make it happen. Her potions helped the process of sex indirectly, but it was never something she had understood as a participant. The unfocused yearnings of her body, particularly strong in the spring when so many animals came together around her in mating rituals, merely amused and puzzled her.

There was nothing amusing about her body's instant reaction to Conlon Maguire. Men had come often to the cottage seeking potions, some handsome, but she had never felt attraction, not even unvoiced admiration for a well-toned body. Of course, perhaps it was Conlon seeing her as she actually looked that roused her awareness of him as a man. Or perhaps it was the blasted potion placing such an unexpected condition on its price that had her focused on her up-until-now dormant libido.

She heard something. A voice, shouting? Marisa emerged in a turbulent wake caused by Conlon's splashing. He had come in to his waist, the water lapping at his hips, his face a worried mask as he called her name.

She paddled toward him, back to where she could stand, the soap in her hand. "It's all right," she said, a bit impatient with him. "I swim here every day." She kept her knees bent as she moved into the shallows so she wasn't exposed.

"I didn't realize it was that deep, and then you just vanished."

His expression softened her. His concern for her showed in his struggle to rein back his anxiety and temper the edge of it in his voice.

"I'm all right," she said. Her gaze flickered to his wet jeans. A shy smile came through despite her efforts to prevent it. "I didn't mean to make you jump in."

The corner of his mouth lifted in a wry gesture she liked. "My own fault. Occupational hazard. Always assume the worst."

He moved forward, lapping the water around her shoulders. Marisa watched him come to her, stared up at him as he put his hands on her upper arms and lifted her.

When she stood, she was in water that wavered at her hips, just above her pubic bone, and the dark hair there could be seen, just below the water's surface. The creek's soft tears slid down her breasts from the silken skeins of her hair resting on her shoulders.

One fingertip reached out, followed the track of a bead of water. It rolled down the outer curve of her breast, under it, over the ripple of her rib cage and past her navel. His thumb brushed that shallow connection to her mother, and every mother of her lineage through her. The drop went into the water, but his hand stayed above the water line, tracing that indentation, the soft but defined rim, and caressed the tiny, tight folds inside. Her stomach contracted under his hand.

"Conlon—"

"Give me the soap."

He took her handmade jasmine-and-orange-scented cake of soap from her hand to lather his hands. He passed the soap back into her palm for he apparently wanted to have both of his hands upon her. Marisa could not dredge up a single protest to the idea.

The water they stood in was mid-thigh level on him. He had gotten the bottom of his shirt wet, so it clung to his abdomen. The wet jeans drew her eye to the way they stretched across his hips and sculpted out the groin area, the weight of his genitals.

His soapy hands started on her hair, working the scent of flowers into it. His touch made it hard to think, but she had spent twenty-three years learning that a person who could not be a part of society had to depend on herself. She had to pull her weight and contribute to the potion's success as much if not more than he did. If she was ignorant, she would have to learn, and learn quickly. There was nothing to be so apprehensive about. Animals, people, everyone did this. It would certainly be easier than learning how to make her own soap, plant a successful garden, or dig her own septic system.

"What do you call your..." She gestured vaguely toward his crotch. At his raised brow, she flushed.

"Well," she groped for his logic, "if I'm going to see it eventually, I should know what you call it. I mean, I know what it's called, but I know...from what you said inside, that you think of these things differently. Stop laughing at me."

He worked his expression from a grin into a suppressed smile.

"That's my cock, Marisa."

"Okay." She closed her eyes as his strong hands massaged the soap into her shoulders. Reaching out to him for balance was hard, but holding on wasn't. She caught her fingers in his shirt just above the waistband of his jeans and rested her wrists on his hipbones.

Sexual longing merged with pure pleasure as his hands worked magic on her shoulders and neck, and she arched, almost purring at the bliss of his soothing touch. Then his hands worked down over her breasts, soaping them, and she caught her lip between her teeth. She breathed through her mouth in shallow spurts as he massaged them, weighed and fondled them, squeezed them until her hold on his shirt became a tight clench.

"A man needs all the cold water he can get around you, Marisa," he muttered, but she didn't open her eyes to ask what he meant, surrendering all senses to his fingertips and what he could do with those hands. He seemed to be able to drive away her worries and rouse her body in this amazing way without disrupting her carefully managed protections. She hadn't known she would be allowed to feel this, not without the pain coming in as well. But a person of pure heart like Conlon didn't have any pain to drive into her.

Her eyes opened when his soapy fingers dipped beneath the water's surface and stroked through her curls, finding her...what did he call it? Pussy, or cunt. She liked the way he said both words. It made her imagine his mouth hovering just above that part of her, coming closer until his lips and tongue were upon the slick folds as he whispered the words. *Pussy. Cunt.* She would open to him, as if those were the words of truth that would win him the right to take all that was there.

His fingers worked the soap over her clitoris, slid down over her opening. She gasped, and her grip moved to tough denim as his fingers worked her, not allowing her to close her legs against the rising, coiling need he stirred, his large hand not permitting her any escape.

"Conlon—"

"You're going to turn this into a hot spring, kitten. Gush your heat over my fingers."

Her toes strained upward, taking her higher out of the water, as if she was trying to get away from his touch, but she didn't want to get away. Something rushed over her, shooting up through her, faster than she could muster a defense against it.

He used her elevated position to get the hand further under her, move the heel of it against her clit. He massaged her in circles as his devilishly knowledgeable fingers played all around the outside of her pussy and dipped within, ticking the base of the clit from the inside.

"No...I...no..." Her hand flailed, splashing hard and awkward into the water. Her feet slipped out from under her, and his arm caught her around the waist, bringing her close and holding her up. The anchor allowed him to keep ruthlessly manipulating her, his fingers the pounding of raindrops beneath the water's surface. The wave of feeling crashed over her, arching her back in his arms. She cried out her passion, a wild lagoon bird, her pale body writhing like a flash of outstretched wings.

"Conlon, please..." She pushed against him and pulled him to her at once as he worked the last spasms through her body. He bent and fastened his teeth on her exposed throat, a gentle, possessive pressure that made her mewl in yearning wonder. The emotional sensation rolled through her, spiraling and twisting together with the physical.

At length he raised his head. She was cradled in his arms, floating, her feet off the ground. His face was all that was in her vision and she could not look beyond him, did not want to do so.

"Let's get you rinsed, kitten," he said, his voice thick, almost violent in its need. "Close your eyes."

His mouth covered hers, and he took them both beneath the water's surface, his body wrapped around her, his fingers moving over her, caressing the soap from her skin, from the soft waving silk of her hair. Marisa held onto him. She'd lost the function of her muscles, including those of her vocal cords.

She didn't need any of them though, for a moment later he was striding from the water, carrying her in his arms, the sun on her bare skin.

"I want to dry you, and then I want to dress you. I want to do everything for you, and to you. I want you to let me. Say yes."

Marisa closed her eyes and turned her face against the pulse beating in his throat rather than answering, making silence her acceptance. She didn't know if her shields were even in place. For the moment, she was dependent on him for protection, and she could only hope he would not be the key to the destruction of her mind she had always feared.

He set her down to dry her off, and she simply held on, unable to stand without his aid. He said nothing, but she felt his attention as if he were speaking a hundred thoughts in her head. She was mute, listening to the rush of whispered images that came through his touch on her body. He lifted her and she simply watched his face, feeling no need to say anything. She closed her eyes when he pressed a kiss to her forehead and then there was a shadow as he crossed the threshold into her house.

He shouldered past the woven cloth dividing her bedroom from the living area, and found where she hung her clothes, behind a curtain she'd made of dried herbs and grasses, giving her clothes the fragrance that clung to her skin.

She didn't have many clothes, and most were sewn by her, simple shift dresses comfortable and appropriate for an old woman. Toward the back, however, was an outfit she had worn only once. It had been a gift from Laraset, the witch who had taught Marisa her craft as well as ways to protect herself. Laraset had been a tarot reader and seamstress on the Renaissance Fair tour before she fell in love with Kohana, a Sioux medicine man. Her gift to Marisa had been a gift of that time in her life, her "time of discovery", she had called it. It was this outfit Conlon lifted out now as Marisa sat naked on the bed watching him, her hair falling around her, covering her breasts and pooling in her lap.

When he turned to her, still clothed in wet jeans and shirt, and her completely naked, she felt even more vulnerable.

"I'd like you to wear this," he said. "I want to see you in a young woman's clothing."

There was a curious lassitude to her limbs and he seemed aware of it, for he laid the clothes on the bed and began to help her dress without asking. He threaded the linen shirt over her head and helped her find the sleeves. It was a peasant blouse with a wide scooped neck. When he slid the velvet skirt over her head and pulled it down to her hips, it tightened the fabric of the shirt over her upper torso. The untied drawstring allowed the neckline to dip so it was just above the line of her nipples. The fabric was transparent. Why that felt more provocative than sitting naked before him, she could not say, but before she could adjust it, he caught her hand.

"No, let me see them," he said. He lifted the last piece of the outfit, a corset to go over the blouse. He drew her to her feet and turned her so she faced the bed, and guided her hands through the armholes. The corset's neckline was even lower than the blouse, and it pulled the softer fabric down further, particularly as Conlon began to work the lacings through the eyelets and tighten the garment around her upper torso.

The binding of the corset felt curiously arousing. She was very conscious that it was his strong hands restricting her in this fashion, almost as if he were binding her to him.

She tried a deeper breath, and her eyes widened as she looked down and saw how close her breasts were to being revealed. The fit of the garment had restricted their space so they had been pressed together and up, as if they were on display for a man's eye. She could see the pale ring of color just above her nipples, and so could Conlon as he turned her around to adjust the points of the corset over her hips. He gazed down on her displayed bosom with full male appreciation.

"You were right to conceal your appearance, kitten," he said, his voice full of heat. "Any man who got a look at you wouldn't take no for an answer."

"Including you?" she asked, raising her chin.

He caught her about the waist and lifted her up above his head so her hair fell down around them, curtaining their faces in an isolated enclave. Marisa caught his shoulders, but more for her balance, for his strength was undeniable, not even a quiver in those arms that held her off the ground. He slowly lowered her until her round breasts were there before his face. His tongue curled over the top of the right areola, tracing its arch, bringing the friction of her bodice and shirt into the blend of textures rubbing over it. He shifted his hold, circling one arm around her waist, the other around her hips. His large palm took a firm grip on her right buttock and he continued his delicate ministration on that one tiny spot of her body, just above a confined nipple that was erect and begging to be in his mouth. He did not heed it, instead tracing his tongue up and over the lifted mounds of both breasts and working a warm, wet path into the dark crevice between them. Her grip slipped from his shoulders, bringing her more fully against his mouth, and she curled her nerveless fingers on his neck, in the dark short ends of his hair.

He raised his head at length, pulling her back from him enough to look at her flushed face. His eyes coursed over the excited heave of her breasts from her arousal and the tight fit of the corset.

"You won't ever say no to me, Marisa," he promised, and she could not argue at the moment, as painful as that possible truth was. Perhaps once her sexual experience quotient was much higher, like a rain gauge, she would be saturated and able to resist someone with Conlon Maguire's magnetism, but by then he would be long gone, wouldn't he?

Something warm and wet was trickling down her thigh and she shifted to press her thighs together. Conlon's brow lifted and he lowered her to her feet. He went down to one knee, which brought his head level with her breasts, and his large hand dipped, lifted the hem of her skirt. Marisa tried to stop him from moving aside the fabric to reveal the tiny drops of fluid that had splashed to the ground. He caught both her wrists in his and held them against her right leg, along with the gathered folds of skirt, as he studied the track of moisture that had run down her left thigh.

"I'm sorry. I need... Let go, and I'll get a towel."

He lifted his gaze to her, and it was brilliant in its intensity. "No."

She sucked in a breath as he bent his head, brought his lip to the point of her knee where the moisture had dropped to the floor. Conlon followed its path back up her leg, using the warm pressure of his tongue and the brush of his soft hair against her bare thighs to loosen them, give him better access as he cleaned the moisture away up over her knee, up her thigh.

He stopped at mid-thigh and lifted his head to look at her flushed face and parted lips. "The flow of your honey tells me what I'm doing to you, Marisa. I like it. It's nothing to be ashamed of. Not ever."

"I'm not." She swallowed. "Why don't... I'll make us some lunch. Would you like something for lunch?"

It was a desperate plea for space and she was relieved

when he smiled and stepped back, though he kept his hands on her, as if to keep her aware of his impending claim on her flesh. She should be offended by his presumption, his easy command of a situation where she was out of her depth, but she couldn't seem to find such an aggressive reaction, not with her physical self so off-balance. Perhaps she had been hit harder than she thought by the rock, and all this was an unusual dream, a dream of things and responses she had not thought possible.

"You may choose to live away from the noise of people's thoughts," Laraset had told her, "but do not close yourself off from your own growth. Don't shut yourself off from the love people will give, no matter how much or how little. Just a moment of love, freely offered, is a powerful magic."

"Let's eat," Conlon said.

Chapter Two

"I don't understand."

He broke off a piece of bread, offered it to her. Marisa took it from his fingers, which brushed and held hers for a moment before they relinquished the food to her. "What don't you understand, kitten?"

"You just..." She shook her head. "I'm sexually inexperienced, yes, and you're overwhelming," she scowled at his grin, "but I'm not stupid."

His smile disappeared. "I don't believe you're stupid at all, Marisa."

"So why are you *really* doing this? This isn't the type of thing a person like you does. I can tell you've given your heart to this woman. How can you—"

Offer me so much that I can't think straight, and yet utterly convince me that you are pledged, heart, mind and soul, to the woman for whom you seek your potion?

His now bare foot moved, curled over her smaller one under the table. "I can't really answer that, Marisa. I trust you, and I trust the potion. Seems to me, if the potion demands a night with you as the price for the woman of my dreams, I should devote my whole heart to it, and to you." He lifted a shoulder, tried out some of the bread, gave a grunt of male appreciation that amused her. He swallowed.

"When you have the True Sight, it takes the guesswork out of decisions. You still have free will, but you don't have the option of rationalizing. You can see what's right and wrong pretty clearly. It may seem to you that our being intimate is a betrayal, but the Sight tells me it isn't. Maybe it's not even about me." He pointed his spoon at her. "Have you considered that the force that guides the potion may have been thinking of *you* this time? Maybe it decided it was time for you to know a man."

Her brow furrowed at the startling observation. He reached across the table, smoothing the wrinkle away, and he winked at her, a curl to his sensual mouth that made the bite of bread she had just taken do a slow somersault in her stomach.

"How did you know you had the True Sight, what it was?"

"Irish gift. My great-grandmother recognized it early on, told me what it was. The family used me more often than the dog to determine if business associates could be trusted, if my sister's boyfriends had honorable intentions." He gave her a wolfish grin that made her own mouth lift in a smile.

"I feel sorry for your poor sister."

"Don't. She married a good man, and she's mean as a pit bull." He took a swallow of water. "Let me ask you something now. How long have you lived here like this, disguised as an old woman?"

"Five years."

"Five years?" He put down his cup. "Marisa, you're only, what? Twenty-one?"

"Twenty-three. I'm twenty-three."

"You've lived here by yourself since you were eighteen years old?"

"I'm not defenseless, Conlon, despite what you saw." Her spine stiffened. "I usually hear visitors coming and can ward the house for intruders. I was just distracted today."

"I don't think you're defenseless, Marisa. But you're alone. Why? Why stay here? Don't you want to travel, to see different places?"

"This is a beautiful place."

"Yes, it is. But home is where you live, not where you hide."

"I'm not hiding," she snapped. "Sometimes people choose to be alone, Conlon. Sometimes that's their destiny."

He reached out, his large hand cupping her resentful

expression. "I don't think it was meant to be yours, Marisa. In fact," his eyes were as fixed and steady as the center of the earth, "I can guarantee it."

She drew back from his touch, refilled both their water glasses from the jug on the floor, quelling the urge to conjure an invisibility spell and vanish. He would see through it anyway.

"Who hurt you?" he asked quietly.

"No one. Everyone." She gritted her teeth at his expression. "I just always have this hope when I travel that I'm going to find a place beyond the cruelty, and there is no such place, not where people exist."

"Maybe it does, you just haven't found it yet."

She inclined her head. "Maybe. I haven't traveled much." *But I can't endure the repeated disappointment of not finding it.* "I think it's much better to watch the Discovery Channel."

"I didn't see your satellite dish."

"I don't have a television here, but I have watched TV," she informed him, suppressing the itch in her palm to slap him. "When you watch a documentary, you know the dark underside exists, but you can filter it, absorb the beauty without being drowned in the darkness. You can at least imagine it might be a wonderful place, instead of a place like any other."

"Sometimes good wins, kitten."

"Yes, and often evil triumphs because the human spirit isn't strong enough to fight it. Or even worse, it can't pay attention long enough to stick with the fight and win it." She propped her elbows on the table with a thump, like a sentry setting the butt of her weapon before a closed doorway. "I don't want to talk about it anymore. My turn again. Have you had to take a life?"

At his startled look, she pointed her spoon at him, mimicking his gesture. "Seems to me," she said, "if you're going to ask me difficult questions, it's only fair that I be able to do the same."

He sat back, eyeing her. "Yes," he said at last. "During a riot in Peru. The mob tried to pull my client out of the car." His expression flickered. "I had to fire into them to break it up, push them back so the driver could get through. I remember the faces of the three men I killed. There might have been more. When you're shooting at close range, it can happen. I fired seven shots."

Marisa reached out, covered his hand. "Oh, Conlon. That must have been awful. I'm sorry."

He lifted a shoulder. "It wasn't one of my favorite days. Truth, kitten, it was probably the scariest moment of my life." He turned his hand and closed it around hers, though his other hand traced the condensation on his glass, his eyes following the track of water there. "There's a claustrophobic heat when you're surrounded by a crowd that's become a mob. Their desire for blood is so strong it presses down on you. It's surreal because the same people a few minutes ago were shopping in the market or talking to neighbors. Suddenly they've transformed into something else. For a moment I thought it wasn't going to be enough to drive them back and we'd be torn to pieces. It didn't work out that way, fortunately. I got Grace Fielding, that was my client, back into the car, and we got out of there."

Her grip tightened on his hand. "You took care of her, brought her home again."

"And thanked every deity of the Western and Eastern world for it because there was no way in hell I did it alone."

"But you still do it," Marisa marveled. "It didn't turn you from it. Did you ever protect someone you felt didn't deserve it?"

"Yes. That's when I left the Secret Service, though I stayed until he left office."

He offered her a bite of bread. He held it away when she reached for it and nodded at her mouth. Marisa hesitated then opened her lips and he placed the bread on her tongue as if she were a baby bird. He withdrew, touching her bottom lip, and then watched the movement of her mouth, the quick flick of her tongue to catch the crumbs. She found it hard to swallow, but she managed it.

"So you don't take on clients not worth protecting."

He nodded. "I spent the first part of my career sometimes having to do that, but once I made enough, I stopped. I only take jobs now that my conscience tells me I should take."

"Where they need the best."

His gaze lifted to hers. "Where someone of my experience is needed. Someone who can be trusted to do the job or die trying. Once I commit to protect someone, I'm there, as long as they need me. If that means forever, then forever it is."

Marisa rose from the table, turned away from him to the basin of water and dipped the bread knife, rubbing her fingers over it to loosen the bread cuttings. "She'll be very lucky, this woman you love," she said, trying to keep the longing for something she would never have out of her voice.

"No, I'll be the lucky one, if she'll have me." He pulled on his hiking shoes, laced them then leaned forward, lifting a wooden spoon out of the arrangement of cooking utensils she kept in a clay pottery piece in the center of the table. "So." He caught her attention by waving it at her. "I think we've both had enough of questions for now. When was the last time you played, Marisa? Other than playing footsy with your cats? When was the last time you played with a human?"

She studied the glint in his eye warily. "You're a little grown up to be playing games, don't you think?"

"Mmmm. Maybe. But you're barely out of girlhood, and I don't think you got enough time to play with dolls or play tag." At her blank look, he lifted a brow. "Tag? One person has to catch the other, then says 'You're it', and gets chased in return? 'Course, it's best played with more people, but if it's just the two of us, I think we can still make it fun." He twirled the spoon's handle in dexterous fingertips. "For instance, say I catch you, I get to bend you over my knee, lift your skirt and spank that pretty bottom of yours with this spoon."

"What? Conlon, you're teasing me. I..."

He rose from the stool, deliberate intent in his sparkling eyes. Marisa was distinctly reminded of Beezle, right before he pounced. A startled laugh bubbled up into her throat. She dropped the knife in the basin, circled left as he dodged right, a grin crossing his features.

"Really," she said, "this is very childish, and—"

"Run, Marisa," he suggested, and lunged after her.

She shrieked and ran through the open door to the yard outside. He was right behind her, but she ducked behind the hedge of roses where a small woman had plenty of room to do her pruning and a large man would be pricked mercilessly. She giggled as she heard him swear. The sound of her mirth shocked her. It spread warmth through her chest and stomach like a special spell. She scuttled to the corner before he could cut her off and headed for the copse of pine and cedar trees that shaded the side and front of the house.

The damn corset restricted her breathing, which suggested a man had invented the thing. She paused, uncertain which way to go. He stalked her, weaving through the same trees, that same menacing grin on his face, the spoon in his hand.

"Now, Conlon." She scampered around a cedar as he made another grab for her, and then danced left as he went the other way. Laughter made her hiccup out words and it felt wonderful. "This is silly."

"Mmm-hmm," he acknowledged, and kept coming. "It's worth it to see you laugh. But, Marisa?" His expression sobered and he came to a stop.

She stopped as well. "What?"

"I've been holding back."

She had time for a short squawk, an aborted dash. He came around the tree, too fast to follow his movements, and had her about the waist, tumbling them to the ground. He rolled so she landed on him, keeping her from harm. It made her body come to a state of high alert, that combination of physical mastery and gentle protection at once. He sat up with her in his lap, turning her face down, not face up, her cheek pressed to the soft earth of the forest floor. The fresh smell of fallen pine needles was there as her fingers curled into them. Panic lighted on her like the tickling brush of falling leaves, and something else, something that sent an instant flood of reaction between her legs.

His hand pressed firmly into her back, holding her

there. The long fingers of that same hand gathered up her skirt, inching the fabric up the back of her legs. Marisa drew in her breath as his hand beneath her body turned and cupped a breast. The play of his fingers on her bare nipple was shocking, making her aware that her position had brought her breasts spilling fully out over the top of the corset.

"Conlon—"

"God, you've got a beautiful ass."

She quivered as the air and the stillness of his hand told her she was fully exposed. Her thighs were draped awkwardly and split open by his knee, so when his hand dipped into the crevice, finding the wetness of her pussy, she could only writhe and whimper helplessly.

"I want to spank you, Marisa. I want to see that pretty little backside you've got thrust in the air turn red and know you'll think of me when you sit down. So hold on." His tone roughened, sending shivers up her spine. "I want it to hurt a little."

Her stomach pressed against his jeans and his cock felt enormous, making her cunt weep for him even further. She was shaking like an autumn leaf unsure when it would lose its connection to its branch. When it let go, the leaf would journey to places never seen before, places that it never imagined existed, except from the fanciful whispers of the wind.

The slap of the spoon on her bottom reverberated to her toes. It hurt, but in a way that made her crave more, craved him to use more of his strength, make her bottom red as he said he would, as if in controlling the response of her skin he was branding her, making her his in truth. Her image of a bookish, quiet man to fulfill her needs was obliterated by the rage of need in her mind, connected to the hand wielding that spoon.

Again. Again. The thwack was loud in the silence. After twenty strokes, the pain got genuine, but he was rubbing her bottom with his broad, gentle palm between each blow, soothing the skin, preparing it for the next. She was weeping, she realized in shock, though her body shivered uncontrollably from pleasure. His blows were drawing forth tears to wash out emotional refuse gathered in the bottom of her heart, things she couldn't understand or name.

By thirty strokes, she flinched at each strike, and he stopped. His fingers stroked her abused skin, and then the spoon's flat, round head was pressing her clit, caressing it. Her blood pressure rebounded, pounding deep in her womb like her clit and pussy had a heartbeat that matched the one thundering in her chest.

The spoon slid to the forest floor and he turned her over, cradling her. She lunged and brought her mouth to his, clutching at his body with both hands. Appeasing her hunger was the only demand in her mind as she attacked his mouth, pulling his tongue into hers, biting his lips, sucking on the moisture and heat of him.

She twisted without breaking the oral contact and wrapped her legs around his waist, depositing her bottom into his wonderful waiting hands. The position brought his cock against her swollen clit. Layers of fabric, the folds of her skirt and his jeans, separated the two, but that did not matter to her straining body. She had no experience, only a complete surrender to the primal urges of her long denied body. She rubbed against him, panting, needing. Just needing. His hands slid up to her hips, pulling her closer, helping her move up and down along his length, though her undulating hips did not seem to need any assistance.

"Don't leave me. Please don't leave me alone."

She heard the words, but it was a full minute before she realized it was she who had said them, pressed them against his mouth.

The realization was as effective as if a hand had picked her up and dropped her in the creek in mid-winter. She shoved back and away, startling him with her abrupt departure such that she was out of his embrace before he could stop her. She scrambled backward several feet and then stopped, the world tilting so she gripped at ground that was no longer steady beneath her.

He'd done it. He was working his way under her shields. She could feel him, feel his desire, his tenderness. Yet he wasn't hers. He wasn't ever going to be hers.

"Marisa—"

"No. *No.* Don't—"

Of course he paid no attention to her. He was beside her, and she shuddered when he touched her.

"It's all right..."

"No, this can't possibly be all right. Don't touch me..."

"That's the problem," he said. "No one's touched you enough." He somehow had pulled her back on his lap and was holding her cradled there. Even stranger was the fact that, despite her protestations, she was holding onto his waist, her cheek pressed against his chest.

"It's okay," he murmured, stroking her hair, letting her sniffle against his shirt.

His comforting hold and his tenderness were as unbearable to her as they were hard to resist.

"This is appalling behavior." Her voice hitched. "I'm sorry."

"Nothing to be sorry for, kitten. Nothing at all. A good spanking works that way sometimes. Hasn't anyone been there for... Don't you have parents?"

She shook her head, kept her hand curled in his shirt, all too aware she was clutching at him the way a child would a parent, for comfort and the reassurance of his presence, the undeniable connection between their life forces.

She knew that humans were social creatures who longed for physical and emotional contact. She had trained herself to do without it because her life depended on being able to stand on her own two feet.

That's what you'll have to do tomorrow, no matter what, her inner demons pointed out slyly. *So why not lean on his strength while it's being offered?*

What if I lose the strength to face the world alone tomorrow?

"Marisa, your parents?"

She sat up, pushed against him. "I need...let me have some space, Conlon. Please."

He reluctantly let her ease into a cross-legged position on the ground in front of him, but he held onto one of her hands. She wiped at her nose and eyes gracelessly with the back of her other one. He found a handkerchief in his pocket and offered it to her, and she used it, hiding behind the action until he put both hands on hers, bringing them and the kerchief back to her lap. "Tell me."

"I wasn't well when I was young, Conlon," she said, focusing on the kerchief to help her say the words. "I had an illness no one could diagnose. I couldn't bear to be touched. The only place I could achieve any type of calm was..." She hesitated, wondering at how difficult it was to say the words. "In an isolated environment, an institution."

His eyes narrowed, his grip tightening. "A padded cell?"

She nodded. "By the time I learned to cope with my problem, I was nearly eighteen, and they hadn't come to see me for years. What was the point? All I remembered was their pain, how helpless they felt.

"When I was five, my mother, she tried to kill herself. That was when my father..." she drew a deep breath to get it out in a rush, "he had to decide. They always made sure I was in the best facilities, that I received the best care. The nurses told me they adopted two children. They were terrified that it was genetic. I sent them a letter when I got out, thanking them for making sure I was safe all those years, but I never could bring myself to go see them. I sent them the letter because I wanted to bring closure to them, to let them know I wasn't angry with them, either of them, that they shouldn't feel they had failed me because they did everything they could."

He tipped her face up, studied it. "You really believe that. You're not just saying it."

She nodded against his hand. "It's difficult for me to live with my...illness at times. How can I blame them? What would I do with a child that always seemed to be in pain when I touched her, who seemed as if she couldn't bear to be in the same room with me? Year after year, with no change."

His eyes were dark with thoughts, his jaw tight. She swallowed, pushed herself onto her own two feet even though the desire to crawl back into his lap was overwhelming.

"You made my bottom hurt," she accused, rubbing the offended area and eyeing him. "Didn't you say once a person is tagged, she gets to chase after the other person and catch *them*?"

At her words, his expression eased a fraction. She reached out a hand, a courteous gesture to help him to his feet. He studied her hand as if the curve of her fingers, the pale skin of her palm were a mystery to him, then he surprised her by placing the spoon in her hand, like a scepter being given to a queen. He rose to his feet. "I did say that."

"Well, I had an unfair handicap with this corset." She tugged it up and wiggled until her breasts were covered as much as they had been before she had landed face first on his lap. When she looked up, she found him watching the play of her breasts with a wry twist to his mouth.

"If you think you had an unfair handicap with the corset, kitten, I think you just balanced it." He caught her hand and before she could guess what he was about, he placed it on the erection starting to swell back hard and firm against his jeans. "Trust me, running with this between your legs isn't easy." His grin flashed wide and bright. "Catch me if you can, kitten. You going to give me a head start?"

She sniffled, swiping away the last evidence of her tears, and tucked the kerchief fastidiously into her skirt's waistband. "If you think you need one."

He bolted and she was after him, her bare feet sure on the forest floor. She had played such games with Beezle, and she knew how to anticipate the feint and double back of a lithe cat's body, but Conlon Maguire had a panther's dangerous grace and the long legs of a giraffe. He widened his lead on her despite her ability to anticipate his movements around the trees, down to the brook, splashing through the shallows, scrambling back up the banks.

She saw no reason to physically compete with those long legs. She concentrated, and a moment later a dead branch on the forest floor spun into his path. He leaped over it, and she gained a stride. A mass of vines fell from the canopy of a water oak and tangled around his shoulders. He got out of that, cursing, but missed the root she pulled several inches out of the ground. He stumbled, and she latched onto the waistband of his jeans and hung on like a small burr. He swung around and caught her deftly about the waist to help her keep her feet.

"You cheat," he laughed. "You witch."

"I am not a cheat," she said with dignity. "I leveled the field between us. You never said I couldn't use magic, and debilitating factors or no," she waved at his crotch, making him grin wider as she flushed, "your legs are much longer than mine, so it was fair for me to do as I did."

"Well then," he drawled, "since we're being fair, do you want me to drop my pants? After all, I gave you your spanking on bare skin."

Her color climbed to her hairline, but she lifted her chin at his teasing, challenging look. "Yes. That's what I want."

His brow raised, but he inclined his head and unbuckled his belt, pulled open the button of his jeans. When she swallowed, and her embarrassed color started to drain from her face, he turned with a cough that might have been a chuckle. He pushed the pants and underwear beneath down to his thighs, and she saw a pair of muscular buttocks, revealed as he gathered up the tail of his shirt. Buttocks that flexed as he shifted his weight to his hip and glanced back at her. "Well, kitten?"

His small witch stood there with the spoon clasped in her hand and a look of something between fascination and terror on her features.

"I just...just..." she stammered. "I just wanted to catch you, to show you I could. I don't need to do...the rest."

"Maybe you'd like to do something else," he suggested, his eyes warm and gentle, but apparently aroused at her innocence as well. "Would you like to touch me, Marisa, any way you wish? Have you ever been able to touch a man's roused body, Marisa?"

"Of course not."

His eyes flamed hotter, surprising her with his reaction. He drew his pants back up, covering himself. He zipped them but left them unfastened and the belt loose and took her hand. "*Good.* Come on."

He led her back into the quiet seclusion of her home, took her through the doorway into her bedroom. He released the tieback on her curtains at the door and windows, so the fabric swung closed, enclosing them in a cozy, dimly lit nest, where there was little room for more than the bed and them, standing there facing each other.

"What do you want, Marisa?" he asked. "Anything. I'll do anything you want. There's nothing we need to rush. Ask me anything."

"Why does it...you seem to like it, very much, that I've never had a man, never touched one," she said. "Why?"

"Because it means I'm the first to know you, that you're mine, that my cock will be the first to fill your sweet cunt, be slicked down with your warm juices when I slide into you." His voice was rich and warm, like the honey he was coaxing from between her legs.

"Oh," she said faintly. The room had gotten much warmer, she supposed because the curtains did not allow as much air to circulate.

"Would you like me to take off my shirt?"

She nodded, and his fingers rose, slipped the second button, the third and the rest. He tugged the shirt out of his waistband and shrugged out of it, baring the broad shoulders and wide chest, the defined muscles that marked his stomach, the low ride of his jeans on his hips.

Living so close to nature, Marisa had a highly developed appreciation of beauty. Whether it was the tiny artistic perfection of a ladybug's wings or the complex symphony of a tree's canopy as the wind brushed strokes through its leaves, she understood each was a miracle. She had never had occasion to study the male form, but that enervated awareness rewarded her now, and for a moment all she did was look. He did not move, letting the dim light settle onto his muscles, limning their perfection for her pleasure.

He was so different. He was so much bigger, not just in height but in the span of his shoulders, the more developed upper body, the size of his hands, the length of his fingers. Small nipples, surrounded by those fine hairs of gilded bronze. The diagonal slashes of muscle from the hip bones, pointing the way to the groin area, still covered by his jeans. Her gaze could not help but settle on that heavy bulge of his genitals contained in the juncture between his long thighs.

"You're beautiful," she said softly. "The most beautiful man I've ever seen."

She moved toward him, and he did nothing, remaining still as he promised, those green-gold eyes watching her. The lack of lighting shadowed his expression, except for the quiet ease of his mouth, inviting her to do as she would to him.

Marisa reached out, and his flesh quivered under her light fingertips. She stroked his fur, felt the texture of his nipple. She took a shallow breath and watched his eyes automatically go to the swell of her breasts, barely tucked back into the tight corset. "I'd like..." she pressed her lips together. Instead of speaking her desire, she reached for it.

She touched the open button on his jeans, traced her finger into the zipper and took it down. She did not look up, absorbed in what she was doing, though she could feel his head bent over hers, his breath on her neck.

"Marisa." It was a husky caress of heat against her skin.

She managed to work the zipper over the head of his engorged cock, moving carefully, instinctively aware of how sensitive that powerful looking organ could be, and noticed the spot of thick fluid on the tip. Fluid like her fluids, wetting his dark underwear as evidence of his desire for her. She could smell it, that musky scent, and it was new to her, so she bent close, inhaled it, breathing softly on him.

"I want..." She wasn't brave enough to go further.

"What, kitten?" His voice was a rough whisper. "Anything you want. Tell me."

"Can you take all of it off?" She straightened, looked up at him. "I want to see all of you."

"I wouldn't know how to tell you no, Marisa."

He bent and unlaced the hiking shoes. As he worked the strings she reached out, traced the movement of his back muscles, felt the soft short hair on his nape. She envied the person who got to cut his hair and run her fingers through it, feel the texture as she was feeling it now. It would be a woman, she was sure, because he was a man who enjoyed the touch of a woman.

He straightened, catching her fingers and kissing them so she did not feel he was drawing away from her touch when he turned to toe off the shoes. He slid the jeans and underwear down his haunches and rid himself of them and his socks, so he stood before her in only the glorious creation of skin and muscle with which the Lord and Lady had blessed him.

He had heavy testicles, covered with the same soft down of dark hair that covered his chest in a light mat, and his cock was fully erect above the scrotal sac. He was large in all ways, and it gave her some trepidation.

She placed her fingers against his rib cage, followed the channel between two of them around to his back, and spread her hand out, a fan against his firm flesh there. She felt the life and strength pulsing within him. "I can barely breathe," she whispered. "You're so wonderful."

A ripple went through his skin and it took her a moment to realize he had swallowed, and his hands had closed into tight fists. She hesitated. "Did I say something wrong?"

"Never." He kept his head averted, but she saw his profile. "You just don't know, Marisa. A virgin in...the outside world, for lack of a better word to call it, is different. She may not have had a man inside her body, but you wouldn't be able to call her sexually inexperienced. She would know so much already. To you, all of it is new, wondrous. It humbles me." He turned then, his body held rigid against some enormous feeling he appeared to be holding back. "A man would look all his life to find someone as special as you. Let me pleasure you while you touch me. I can't keep my hands off you."

"How?" she asked, not certain of his intent but certain she would not deny anything he asked of her in that ragged voice.

"Come here." He drew her to the bed and stretched his long body out on it, laying his head on her pillow. If he stayed there long enough, she'd be able to smell him long after he was a memory. She was glad she had made the bed oversized for her and all of the cats because his feet were almost at the bottom railing.

"Come here," he repeated, tugging at her, at her skirt.

He pulled the drawstring, untied it and loosened its fit, so the skirt went tumbling to her ankles, leaving her only in the corset and shirt beneath. He took her elbow, guided her up onto the mattress and then brought one of her legs over his chest to straddle him, with her head facing his feet.

"What—"

He slid her back, his hands on her thighs, and she was on her knees, her hips over his face, her hands braced on the bed on either side of his rib cage.

"Touch me however you wish, Marisa," he told her, his hands closing on her waist as she tried to twist about and look at him, "while I bring you pleasure this way."

She understood then, and before she could become embarrassed or ask desperate questions, he brought her down full on his face, her pussy onto his waiting mouth.

It was like the exhilarating shock of cold water on a very hot day. Pleasure shot out in all directions through her bloodstream from that point of contact between his mouth and her body. She couldn't think of a proper analogy for it, the feel of a man's hot, hungry mouth on her wet, aroused cunt. He flicked his tongue back and forth like the lash of Beezle's tail, then around in a circle. She struggled, not to get away, just unable to be still. He seemed to understand, for he held her more tightly. His tongue made a slow, broad lick, from back to front, up and down, again and again, all while he made soft, wet sucking noises against her skin that inflamed her body and her senses.

Marisa fell forward, unable to sit upright, and found a feast waiting for the ravenous hunger he roused in her. She opened her own mouth and used it upon him. She started with his flat stomach, using her teeth to taste the roll of muscles there, biting and licking wildly like Beezle did when she scratched his back and hit the spot he liked so much. If it felt anything like this, she now knew why he got more and more aggressive as the pleasure continued building, until the best expression of appreciation was savagery.

Conlon used his greater strength to show her how to enhance her pleasure, manipulating her hips in low grinding circles, allowing him to stab his tongue deeper into her heat.

Her arms stretched, her fingers biting into the tops of his thighs. She sucked on his hipbone. His tongue stabbed deep and she mewled, curling her claws into him, her knees straining to clamp onto either side of his head. His hands held her wide, so her body shuddered in the grip of an unbearable level of arousal, unable to go forward, screaming to be pushed over that pinnacle he had shown her in the water. Her clit was aching for his mouth, but now when she wanted it most, he offered only the smallest rations to that aroused center. A brief nuzzle, a quick lick. She cried out at the teasing contact, throwing back her head.

His cock brushed her cheek and her hand slid back to the crease between thigh and testicles. Marisa turned her head and rubbed her nose and the edge of her lips against the broad head, tasting wetness and salt. She marveled at the peculiar velvet softness of skin stretched over steel.

Conlon settled into a rhythmic nursing at her pussy, so slow it felt as if her cunt were the eye of the storm raging through her body. Every slight movement of his mouth and every hot breath were as excruciating as an electric jolt.

She was quivering, her breath sobbing in her throat, and she tasted him again, more boldly, running her tongue along the ridged base of the head of his cock. She used a hint of teeth, as he had on her. He groaned against her slickness, and the convulsive clutch of his fingers on her thighs told her he liked it.

She cupped her hand under his testicles, feeling their weight, and licked his cock again from the base up to the tip. She wanted to hold it, this staff that would take her maidenhead, and so she wrapped her fingers around it. She slid her grip up, feeling the unusual give of the soft flesh over firm rigidity. It had incredible heat, warming the skin of her palm. She rose up and put the head fully into her mouth, just barely able to close her lips over it, touching it lightly inside the cavern of her mouth with little flicks of her tongue, learning his contours.

He stilled, his lips motionless on her pussy but still *there*. His fingers lightly stroked the inside of her thighs, making her tremble even more.

He was very thick. Her index finger and thumb were barely able to meet as she grasped him to slide her mouth further down on him. She went as far as she could go before the head touched the back of her throat. His thighs quivered, just a shiver of movement, but it flooded her with a sense of power. She could do to his body what he did to hers, make him helpless with pleasure. She slid back up his length, feeling the way he stretched her small mouth, and she used her teeth, scraping, and sucked on his skin.

"No, Marisa..." His breath rasped hard over the words, and she felt his heart pounding beneath her thighs. "You'll have to stop, or I'll be no good to you at all."

She shook her head, made a murmured protest, her mouth still firmly fastened on him. She had no intention of relinquishing her new toy. He answered her willfulness with his mouth. He clamped his lips back over her soaking cunt, only this time there were no gentle licks or nibbles to draw out her pleasure. His hands shoved her thighs impossibly wider, and he suckled her clit hard. He lifted her hips off him and then drew them back down in a pumping motion, to give his tongue room to stab in and out of her labia, emulating the act they would eventually do with the organ in her mouth. He alternated the sucking of her clit and the invasion of her pussy with his tongue with long, thorough licks from the top of her clit to the tiny opening of her bottom. He stabbed back into her pussy on each downward stroke, an amazing feat of coordination that shot her up a ramp toward orgasm like a slalom skier. His afternoon beard rasped against her delicate skin, tightening the coils in her lower belly impossibly further.

The banked heat while she explored him now leaped high. She whimpered, her mouth still upon him, but unable to coordinate a sliding motion to tease him as he was tormenting her. In fact, she could do little other than hang on, her hands clutching his legs, her mouth panting on his cock, vibrating it with her soft cries. The head bumped the back of her throat as he mercilessly undulated her body toward a shattering peak.

"No...no..." She did not know why she was saying no,

denying him, except it felt like too much, too frightening and overwhelming. The power that grew in her pussy coiled in her lower belly with the power of a diamondback about to strike, and then it did, in a blinding flash as brilliant as venomed fangs. She saw hues of silver and light sparking in the back of her eyes as his teeth scraped her convulsing clit, consuming her heat and juices as if he dined on a meal of flesh prepared just for him. Indeed, at the moment she could not imagine belonging to anyone else but him.

She could accept that, would have to accept that. As unlikely as it had been more than a couple hours ago that he would be her first love, Conlon Maguire would likely be her last, with her life being what it was. She let go and was ripped away from the edge of reason, spiraling into the world of silver, her cheek pressed against his thigh for she could hold her mouth on him no longer. He continued to drive her higher even as she begged him for mercy. His arms were banded on her waist and hips, and his mouth worked her hard, bringing forth a primal passion and need she had not suspected were there, stored like a thousand unshed tears in her subconscious, just like the emotions released by his spanking. She sank her teeth into his flesh and the blood of his thigh gave her the anchor she needed, her cheek pressed against the heat of his erect cock and nest of testicles.

The pounding rhythm of his blood matched hers, but hers slowed first as she came down. She focused on herself with wonder, feeling the way her climaxing body contracted on his tongue, then pulsed down to an easier cadence, like a settling heartbeat. His hunger became a nibbling, just a feather touch of his mouth that made her wriggle a bit against his hold as the sensitive tissues were tickled.

His hands at last let her go but only to lift and turn her.

"Come up here, Marisa," he murmured. "Taste your pussy on my mouth."

She let his hands guide her so she lay full on him, his cock trapped between her belly and his, her response trickling down her thigh onto his leg.

He lifted her under the armpits, slid her up to where he could kiss her, which meant his cock sprang up between her thighs and nudged the crease between her buttocks.

His mouth was warm and gentle, and she could taste his leashed need beneath the flavor of her cunt, a slippery, exotic taste. His hand came up and cradled the back of her head, his thumb stroking her ear. She loved how he liked to touch her face when he kissed her. She was reduced to a still peace by his gentleness, and a desire that was more than physical, though she could feel a stirring in her lower belly. She felt like a languid cat who had enjoyed her supper so much, she might want more sooner than expected.

"Conlon," she whispered, shyly meeting his gaze. "I'd like to take off the corset so I can feel all of you against me."

His fingers worked the laces free and the pressure eased. She sat up so he could pull the garment away, leaving her soft and bare sitting upon him. As she sat up, she lifted her body so his cock came forward through the opening of her thighs and lay on his belly again. When she lowered herself, she found it nestled against her pussy, the long hard length of him channeled between her wet lips.

Conlon reached up, fondled her breasts, rubbing his thumbs over her still aroused nipples. "Holy Mother, I want you. Can you feel how much, kitten?"

She thought he meant his cock beneath her, but he took her hand, laid it over his heart and held it there as he stared up at her through the dim light.

Blessed Lady, what was the man trying to do to her? When she started this day, she could not have imagined she would be sitting on a naked man by late afternoon, but here she was, and now he seemed determined to crack open her insides the way he had pushed past her physical defenses.

He had roused powerful emotions in her, and perhaps that was what happened during sex. For just a few moments, you got to be everything to one another, even if you were nearly strangers. She had never been anything special to any person, not for a second, much less for an afternoon, so how could she resist it? This moment was a gift, a memory she could polish every day so it would not dim, like a lamp in her soul. She had always accepted darkness there, but she was afraid he had made it impossible for her to accept it anymore.

"I want you to..." She paused, her fingers resting beneath his, her other hand holding her up on his body. She loved the way his eyes coursed over her, again and again, as if he was trying to memorize everything about her, and then his gaze returned to her face, studying it with equal intensity. "Do you say 'have sex with me'?" she asked.

She had certainly read books, but she had stayed away from modern literature. It was a world she could not join, and so reading those books caused her only longings for things she could not have. Her naivete and innocence were real things, her questions to Conlon genuine, his every answer a new wonder for her to ponder.

He reached up, cupped her face in both of his hands, bringing her down for a kiss on her forehead, her nose. The tips of her breasts brushed his bare chest, making them tingle.

"Sometimes," he murmured, kissing her lips, "when you especially want it, and there's just an overpowering physical need inside you, you say, 'I want you to fuck me. Now.'" His lips brushed over her brow again. "Hard." Her ear, to nibble. "Long." Back to her lips, this time for a much longer kiss, during which her world spun off its axis and drifted away on a cloud.

"Then," he raised her face and she caught hold of his wrists to keep her balance, staring into his eyes, "sometimes it's more, so much more, and you say, 'make love to me'. Say that to me, Marisa. Please."

She closed her eyes, turned her face into his hand, pressed her temple there. "I can't," she whispered. "You're going to leave. You can't take everything from me, Conlon. You can't." She brought her gaze back around to him, her lips trembling. "Fuck me, Conlon." She stumbled over it, but she drew a breath and strengthened her resolve. "Fuck me. Now. Hard. Long. Make me yours for today, and I will live with that, if you can, and your potion will be served."

The last was a challenge, and her anger surprised her. It wasn't supposed to have gotten personal, but it had because there was no way to get this close physically without it becoming that way, a painful lesson she would not forget. She didn't have the experience to be casual about it. He did, but his husky words, begging her for verbal intimacy, had not sounded casual. Neither was his reaction now.

There was a flash of frustration, a deep disappointment that made her want to withdraw, break the physical link of flesh with him, but he stopped her, his fingers biting into her arms. He pulled her down, put his forehead against hers, and she kept her palms open and light against his chest as he fought a battle for control she could feel quivering through his body.

"Before we do that," he said at last, "we need to take a little break. Your body will need some time to get roused again, to make certain you can receive me as comfortably as possible. After climax, the tissues are very sensitive, too sensitive."

"I can bear it," she assured him.

He shifted his grip and collared her throat, giving her a hard look that swallowed anything else she had intended to say to goad him to finish, to be done with it.

"I won't let you rush this, Marisa. You'll open every part of yourself to me, not compartmentalize to protect yourself. You never need to do that with me."

Didn't she? Why did he act as if he was not going to leave her when the day was done? Why did he want her to act the same way?

He gave her ass a friendly squeeze as if he had not just insisted she put her heart in his hands.

"Right now," he lifted her off him, putting her on her feet on the floor next to the bed, "I need to answer the call of nature."

She knew they were serving a Will greater than her own desires, but he irritated her beyond the capacity for speech. She wanted to tear out her hair, or better, his. As he rose and turned to leave her small bedroom, she snatched up the spoon and gave him a solid whack on his muscular ass.

Conlon jumped and spun, shock flashing over his expression for one delightful, vindicating moment. Then a wicked grin crossed his face. "You're going to wish you hadn't done that."

Marisa dropped the spoon and bolted, but he snatched her by the waist and hefted her over his shoulder kicking and shrieking. She used her hands and smacked him again, taking out her frustration with a cheerful enthusiasm on his handsome backside all the way from inside her house to the creek. By the time they got to the water, she was laughing at his mock sounds of pain and missing every other blow. He tried to lift her, she was sure to toss her into the water, but she wrapped her arms around his neck and her legs around his waist as he brought her forward. "I'm not going in unless you are," she informed him.

"All right then," he said, and plunged in with her locked in his arms. He took four strides and dove below the surface of the deeper water.

It was marvelous, having him hold her, water rushing over them both. Even when he rose, she continued to cling, water pouring off their naked bodies, the melting afternoon sun warming their skin as they emerged. Beezle sat on the bank, watching them with yellow eyes rounded in amazement.

"Kitten, you've got quite an arm." He grinned, pushing her hair back from her face as she did the same to him, smoothing it back on his temples. "You'd be a hellcat of a mother."

The light in her heart died, and he saw it, for his face sobered. "What, Marisa?"

"I'll never have children, Conlon. My...problem, it makes it impossible."

"I thought you said it was cured. Is it life threatening?" He gripped her arms. "Are you sick? Tell me."

"No, I said I learned to manage it. It's not something you cure."

"Why won't you tell me what it is?" He gave her a firm shake. "I want to help."

"No." She shook her head. "Please don't ask me to talk about it. It's nothing that threatens my life, not that way. I just want to swim. Go...do what you need to do, and let's swim. Okay?"

She was grateful when he let her pull away, when he didn't push. She knew how difficult that was for a man who wanted to protect all those around him and remembering that, she resigned herself to the fact that she couldn't seem to hold onto her anger against him.

She knew Conlon did not mean to upset her with his insistence that she open herself to him. He did not know how susceptible her emotional wellbeing was. He was simply encouraging her to offer herself fully to the passion between them.

When he splashed back into the water, his face was more composed.

"Come on." He retrieved her hand, pulling her into the deeper water, beyond where her feet could touch. "Keep me company out here."

He let her go and sank below the water then came back up, tossing his hair out of his face. He could touch bottom here, the water lapping at his collarbone, so she stroked over to him. His fingers linked with hers and he pulled her in, guiding her thighs so they wrapped around his waist and she could use him to keep herself afloat without treading. His waist was firm beneath her soft thighs, the hair on his belly brushing and tickling the hair of her pubic mound. Her calves pressed down on his muscular buttocks, her crossed heels resting on the backs of his thighs. She realized if they were lying down, this would be the position of coitus, and it turned the emotions fluttering in her stomach to liquid heat.

"I can see why you live here," he acknowledged, looking around them. "It is peaceful. But don't you get lonely, Marisa?"

"Sometimes." She used her arms to keep herself upright, her upper body leaning away from him. "But I have Beezle and six other abandoned cats that come here to eat."

"Who built the house?" He studied the simple log cabin construction.

"I did," she said, with some pride at his look of surprise. "I studied survivalist manuals, everything from Robinson

Crusoe to Walden Pond, and modern journals. Especially those written by women. Then I just followed the blueprint of what they did. Laraset and Kohana are the healers who helped me learn how to cope with my illness and got me to the point where I could leave the care of a medical facility. They're married, and they came with some of Kohana's cousins and helped with the heavy lifting when I was constructing the cabin."

"Why didn't you stay near them? If Laraset and her husband helped you reclaim your life, they must be good friends."

"They were my healers." She nodded, tightening her thighs on his bare hips as he shifted. "They cared about me as physicians care for those they heal. But I spent my whole life under medical care, Conlon. I wanted to see what it was like to have my own home and my own life, as much as I could. My parents set up a trust fund for me so I could choose where to live and what to do with my life and have whatever level of care I needed."

"But you're so isolated here."

"Not so much." She shrugged. "People like you are company, those who come here looking for potions. I go into town," she added, laying her head back in the water to float her upper body, though she continued to hold onto him with her legs. "I see people then."

"Well, it's obvious how often you go there." The flatness of his voice had her raising her head. "All the window shopping for trinkets, the pretty dresses you buy."

"I don't stay that long." She dropped her legs from their hold around his hips and swam away, rolling in the water, rewetting her shoulders. He swam alongside her.

"You strike me as someone who would enjoy looking at lovely things, Marisa. Trying on a pair of earrings, a hair comb. Do you go in as yourself? Or do you go in as an old woman to keep anyone from noticing you?"

"Stop baiting me," she snapped.

She had retreated enough that she was back on solid ground and she faced him, anger in her eyes. "You want to hear what you're fishing for, Conlon? I go to town once a month, for about two hours. That's what I can handle, okay?"

"Until what?" He stood up, his shoulders broad enough to block the sun setting behind him, making the wind raise a chill on her upper arms a moment before his hands closed on them. "Tell me what happens, Marisa."

"Why do you insist on making this about me?" she said, jerking away from him. "This is about *you.* Your potion, your life, your woman. I will never see you again after today. I am an instrument of other people's fates, not part of fate itself."

She saw it in his face. Pity. Pity for her. Marisa snarled and she spun away from him. "We'll do this *now,* and then you and your potion can be gone."

He caught her about the waist and she whirled on him like a cat, clawing at him. He caught her wrists and she resorted to teeth, snarling at him, fighting the needs he had roused. Needs that exposed her terrible isolation and the inadequacies of the world she had been forced to create to survive.

"Marisa—"

"Bastard!" She wrenched away from him. "You pry and pry because you think I'm interesting and different, because I'm beautiful, but you don't live in my head every day. You don't know what it's like to live in fear of the pain coming back, the constant hammering of a million dark voices raised in threats, anger and pain until you can't hear the voice of a good person standing next to you shouting. Do you have any idea how shielded I must be to survive? How much effort it takes every day to hold those shields in place? And you come here with your patronizing attitude and your sexist assumption that I'm some weak, stupid female."

"Marisa, no—"

"You want to know what happens if I stay in town longer?" Her lip curled derisively. "My shields break down and all the ugliness pours in. Everyone's meanest, most petty thoughts and deeds, the things deep in their heads that no one knows about."

"Jesus. You're an empath." The light dawned in his eyes.

She nodded, a short, sharp jerk. "Yes. A *very* special

type of empath, Conlon. I only sense emotions motivated by evil. And guess what? Almost all of us have them, even if they're dormant within us. I can sense them. Greed, petty selfishness, unjustified violence, the dark yearnings that everyone harbors deep inside. You know those primal instincts that turn a group of pleasant shoppers into a murderous mob? Well, I feel it in them in the marketplace, while they're still shopping, even if all they ever do is shop." She set her jaw to keep her voice from trembling. "Only the shields I've learned to build protect me, and the moment I come into town it's like my mind is a fortress under siege by an army. Those with true Darkness in the active part of their minds make it far worse."

He reached out but she shook her head, stroked back from him. "That's why I spent all those years in an institution. Can you imagine being a child, and all these terrible images are pounding into your head from everyone you know? It's like one of those horror movies, where people look normal, but you're seeing them as demons, their innermost gremlins exposed on their faces, in their voices."

"Oh, Marisa."

"Laraset was a volunteer in the children's ward. She's a witch, and she brought her husband Kohana to see me. He's a Sioux medicine man, and he figured out what I was, looked beyond the physical and chemical to the spiritual. They helped me, helped me learn how to shield myself for short forays among others and taught me the things I needed to do to cope. One of them is living apart from civilization, where I can keep it down to just a murmur of static in my head."

"There's no permanent cure for it."

Somehow, she knew he was going to ask. "There's only one permanent solution for it, a reference in a book that might or might not be true. When Laraset found it and told me about it, I wished for it so much I almost put myself back in the same state again. Just like the shields, I learned to protect myself by not wishing for it anymore."

Liar. His presence here had brought it to the surface like a predator floating in the shallows, just waiting for her fragile psyche to put one vulnerable leg into those dangerous waters.

"You won't tell me what it is?"

She shook her head. "I don't speak of it. I won't. I can't." She could not keep the desperate note from her voice.

"And the potions?" he asked quietly.

"An act, a joining of love, eases the drain on my shields. The success of my potions, no matter how far away, fuels the wards around this place, around me."

"So your potions are for you as well as for them."

"They make the world a better place, so everyone wins." She set her jaw. "I live alone and maintain my wards and my illusion and I survive. It's the life I have been given, and it has many blessings in it."

"Marisa." He reached beneath the water, caught her hand and stepped closer. His other fingers touched her chin, lifting it so she would meet his intense hazel gaze. "You don't have to tell me what you and Laraset found, but I know faith grows weak. I know it." His hand tightened on her, and she saw the truth in the shadows of his eyes. "My faith nearly broke after Peru. I never thought that kind of darkness was in people. But I learned that as long as your faith is still inside you, even just a thread of it in your heart, it can call your heart's desire to you if your intent is pure. You have to believe."

"I have to survive," she said flatly. "And enjoy what I've been given rather than always wishing for what I can't have." A man in her life exactly like Conlon Maguire. "Anyway, by nightfall, I'll no longer be such a pure vessel, will I?" The porous ground beneath her feet sucked her down, sliding her closer to him, despite her struggle to pull back.

"Innocence is not purity, Marisa," he said seriously. "Physical intimacy doesn't taint the soul. In some cases, it can enhance the shine." He drew her closer so her breasts and her stomach were pressed against his wet skin. She had to tilt her head to look at him, which put their mouths distractingly close. "You have every right to be proud. I wasn't trying to pick that apart. You just have an incredible amount to give, Marisa." His hands slid up her sides, palms resting on her rib cage. "I wish there was someone in your life with whom you could share it all. Not someone to nurse you. Someone to be with you, be your helpmeet. Share your life."

"You think I don't wish for that?" she demanded, stiffening against his hold. "Laraset said..."

"What? What did she say?"

"She said that maybe one day I'd find someone." There, she'd said it. "Someone who might get close enough to me that they could lend their strength to my shields. But it can't be just anyone. So it's impossible."

He opened his mouth to respond, but she'd had enough. Marisa wrenched away. "You see, you've got me messed up about this again. You're just like Laraset, always pushing, always wanting me to offer more. Well, none of you are in my head. It isn't about what all of you want me to be able to do, it's what I can do to serve the Lord and Lady and still survive from day to day. So as far as I'm concerned, the whole bunch of you can just go to hell. This is my life."

She stormed out of the water, leaving him there, and snatched up her towel from the basket. She wrapped it around herself and plopped down on the bank, deciding he could finish his bath alone, and if he got his legs tangled in some water weeds and started to drown she might just wait awhile before deciding to fish him out.

After a few minutes he joined her. She chose not to look at him, though she couldn't help her peripheral vision, which noted the way the sunlight played off the water sluicing down the muscles of his body, the dark pelt of pubic hair, the movement of his genitals as he strode from the water. He picked up the other towel she had provided and knotted it loosely on his hips. He sat down next to her, joining his hands around his bent knees.

"If you were one of your cats, your tail would be lashing and your ears would be laid back."

Her gaze shot to his face. She could feel the fire inside her shooting sparks from her eyes, but his expression was open and apologetic. "So," he ventured, "want to have sex now?"

The anger slid away with her glare and she looked away,

her lips twitching. "Idiot."

"Yeah, it kind of goes with the whole male-female dynamic." He carefully laid an arm around her shoulders and she felt his warmth, the comforting touch of something she'd rarely had, a friend.

"I didn't really mean I wanted you to all go to hell," she said after a moment.

"Even me."

"Even you. I did kind of want you to drown, for a second or two."

He chuckled and she laid her head on his shoulder, let herself lean for just that moment because, after all, once the moon rose, it wouldn't matter.

"Does that mean I can talk you into having dinner with me?"

"Didn't we just eat?"

"That was a snack. This is dinner."

"What are you fixing?" she asked, a smile touching her lips, curving against the skin of his shoulder.

He nudged her so she lifted her head.

"You tell me what you have, and I'll make it into something worth eating. I'm a great scratch cook."

She considered. "Well, I've got fresh vegetables, bread and..." she slanted him a glance, "Hershey chocolate bars. A case of them, one a day to last me until my next trip into town."

"My God, you've fallen in love with me."

"What?" She jerked back.

"A woman doesn't offer her chocolate stash to someone she's not madly in love with."

"Perhaps I just have a generous nature," she said, recovering her dignity.

"I've no doubt you do about most things, but a woman and her chocolate? Kitten, you'd be the first."

He grinned and rose, offering her a hand. When he tugged her to her feet, he brought her close, so her towel-clad body was pressed against his bare upper torso. She was suddenly aware of how loosely that towel draped about his lean hips. But he stepped away after a moment and just held her hand as they walked back to her house.

Chapter Three

"Play 'what if' with me."

"You don't play 'what if' if there's no possibility you can ever have what you're wishing for."

"With all you do to ensure the success of your potions, you don't think anything's possible?"

"Are you trying to be cruel?"

"I want you to share your dreams with me, kitten. That's all."

Marisa studied him across the table. He had indeed prepared an excellent meal, concocting a spicy light soup of vegetables from her garden. She had sliced up more of her wonderful bread. Now they faced each other, and the candles she had lit upon the table were becoming necessary to illuminate the room, every flicker of the flames like the ticking of a clock, tightening a coil of anticipation in her belly. She saw the awareness in his eyes as well, though they kept up their conversation as if they were both oblivious to the significance of the impending twilight.

"It's more than the empathy that makes me choose isolation. I'm not a prisoner of this place, Conlon. The noise of towns, the way no one pays attention to the natural world except as an accent to their possessions, it's not for me. Here, I'm connected to the Lord and Lady, as part of the cycles around me, and I can hear Their Voices and my own."

"So that's why no electricity."

"I don't need it." She shrugged. "People get far too dependent on such things anyway."

"Hmmm." He rose, collected the dishes and deposited

them in the basin of water in a considerate gesture that had as much of an impact on her senses as the physical implications of the moon rising. It made her think of his words.

Someone to be with you, be your helpmeet... Someone to share your life.

Someone to share mundane tasks like washing the dishes. Another person to stand on the other side of the wide bed in the morning and help her make it. Someone to help her take a jar off a shelf just out of reach of her fingertips.

He lifted his backpack to his shoulder and extended his hand. "I think it's time, kitten. Will you come to the bedroom with me?"

Her throat suddenly went dry, but she nodded, rose and took his hand, let him lead her into the bedroom.

Conlon set the backpack down. "Will you lie back on the bed for me, Marisa?"

They had worn their towels at the table. His clothes were wet and he did not want her to put on one of the shift dresses. She lay back on the pillow and pressed her cheek to it as he rummaged through the bag. She smelled him on the pillow, just as she'd hoped.

She opened her eyes to find he had removed a small item of pale blue rubber, shaped like a butterfly. He was using his fingertip to spread a fluid from a tiny bottle onto the butterfly's wings.

"What is that?"

He sat down on the bed next to her hips and slid his hand holding the butterfly up her thigh, nudging the terry cloth out of his path so her leg from knee to pussy was exposed to his gaze. "Spread your legs for me, kitten," he murmured. "I have a surprise for you. Courtesy of the Eastern invention of the alkaline battery."

She trembled but obeyed, trusting him in a way she knew she had never trusted anyone.

His fingers touched her, pressed her gently, and the wings of the butterfly closed over her clit, the substance he had spread onto them adhering to her skin so it stayed in place, like a hood for the tiny bundle of excited nerve endings.

"What is it?" she repeated again, breathless.

"Something to change your mind about electricity."

The whir of the tiny motor was almost noiseless, but its impact was immediate. Marisa stiffened as the vibrations kissed her clit, little frissons of current drawing the blood so it began to swell in arousal again.

"Ah." She caught her lip in her teeth as he watched her, his eyes steady on her face, his hand on her thigh, his fingers achingly close. His hand held the control at his hip and he turned the knob. She bucked up as the sensation intensified.

"Your nipples are hardening," he said quietly. "They have jewelry for them, did you know? Rings to go around them, make them stay stiff and large. There are even vibrating shields for them so they can become as aroused as your clit is now. I can turn this up to its highest setting and you'll come instantly, Marisa. You're getting wetter even now. I can smell it. You're ready for it again."

"Conlon." She clutched the covers, sensations shuddering over her skin. She opened her legs wider, lifted her hips toward him. She felt like a wanton, wanting to offer all of herself to him, but she couldn't help it. From the flare of heat in his eyes, she could see he didn't mind.

However, he turned the control down, easing the vibrations so she could think somewhat again, and stroked his hand down her trembling leg. "You could come that way, but I want you to come this time with my cock inside of you. It's just about dusk," he murmured, glancing toward the open window.

The crickets were starting their evening serenade, and the air had the soft quality of early summer evenings. It was a lovely time of day to embrace a change to her life, for she knew that was what this was. The price of the potion was never set without deep purpose, and the amethyst color, the color of the crown chakra, had underscored its significance.

"Conlon, could you... Would you mind stopping it just a moment? I have to... It's important I tell you something."

He acquiesced to her wishes and even went a step

further, leaning forward to take the butterfly off her. The touch of his fingers peeling it off her clit was enough to make her gasp, her thighs tighten. He bent, pressed a kiss to her pubic bone, nuzzling her soft hair, then he straightened, met her gaze.

"Are you afraid?" His voice was soft, though she could feel the tension in his man's body, the ache of wanting her so close to the surface it emanated from his skin. It helped, knowing that.

"Not of the act. Just of what it might mean. Conlon." She pressed her lips together. "It's possible, when we come together, that I won't be able to maintain my shields. Great emotion widens the scope of my empathy and..." She stopped to steady her voice, felt his hand close on hers. "I know this will overwhelm me. If the negative emotions rush in, promise me you'll finish the consummation, no matter how much pain I appear to be suffering."

His expression hardened. "I'm not going to cause you suffering, Marisa. If there's any danger to you, we're not going to do this. I don't care what—"

"No, it's important to the magic that sets the price that we come together in this way. I wish to serve its purpose. Please, you must promise me, despite your strongest instincts, to do this."

It was she who turned over her hands and gripped his hard, her expression beseeching. "I serve the Lord and Lady. Don't deny me the right to control my own destiny. That's far more important to me than anything else, do you understand?"

He studied her. "All right," he said at last. She knew it cost him to go against his own inclinations to support hers and she lifted his hands to her mouth, kissing them.

"I will do as you say," he warned her, "but I will do everything I can to keep you safe. You'll have to be satisfied with that."

Would he talk to his chosen woman so possessively, so arrogantly? Marisa closed her eyes and imagined that woman's lips lifting in an indulgent smile as his hands and mouth and words asserted his dominance over her, all the while knowing she held his heart and soul in her gentle hands. It was the way of the Lord and Lady, the unique way male and female expressed their sense of belonging to one another, their mutual reverence and devotion. She understood it now, after only one afternoon with a man. Not just any man, but the right man, to teach her such truths.

She nodded, not trusting herself to speak further. He drew her forward, into his arms, all the way in, pressing her into the curve of his body so she was sheltered there. He wrapped his arms around her back so she was in a cavern of male heat and strength. He tipped her chin back with a nudge of his jawline, and he kissed her.

They'd had a whole afternoon of loveplay, so she had anticipated that he would quickly move to the intimacy of baring both their bodies again, stripping away the towels, claiming her breasts and thighs with his mouth and hands.

Instead, he seemed to want to take his time now, seducing her only with his mouth. He started with a persuasive rubbing of his lips against hers, pushing her bottom lip down with the pressure of his so his lips were moistened by the inside of hers. He rubbed that moisture against both of her lips. The tip of his tongue came out, making a delicate touch here and there, as if he was marking each tiny crease of her lips that enabled their movement. Marisa's fingers uncurled and fluttered onto his abdomen, pressing against his hot skin. She caught the light covering of hair there, a reflexive clutching for balance as he took hers away.

Her lips parted, welcoming him deeper, but he would not take the plunge. His tongue touched the edge of her bottom front teeth, delicate licks to her gum line, his large hand coming up to hold her jaw still for him.

She made a noise at the back of her throat, and her body pushed against his, insistent.

"Tell me you want me to make love to you, Marisa," he said, his harsh whisper no less a demand because it was a heated breath along her cheek. "This is not sex, not fucking. No matter what happens after this night, you know that's the truth. You serve the truth and love. Let me in. Trust me for this one moment, the most important moment in the world."

The hard-won mental wall she had built crumbled like a sandcastle against the onslaught of the ocean, just from those few coaxing words. His strength and goodness surrounded her, made her feel desired and protected, revered and enjoyed at once.

Marisa now understood why desperation for this feeling bloomed in the many hearts that visited her door. This was the greatest of magics. Even if a person had never had this blissful feeling herself, the sacred Joining of the Lord and Lady to renew the cycles of life emanated outward and encompassed all Their creations. All who were a part of Their Body would feel those emanations and long to have it for themselves, be a part of it. As above, so below, as within, so without. It could be measured in an hour or a second, but it would never be enough until it became a state of existence, an infinite instead of a finite experience.

"Yes." She looked up at him, his beautiful, handsome spirit, the desire waiting to be unleashed in his eyes, his hands, his cock moving against her. "Make love to me, Conlon."

She gave a glad cry as he plunged, mating their mouths in a full penetration, his hands moving down to hold her hips firmly against him.

He slid onto the bed, covering her body with his own. She lay down in the comfort of this bed every night. Lying down in it now, with his body settling on top of hers, felt more welcome than the best dream she had ever known in it. Her thighs opened to cradle his body, and her towel slid to the floor as he unknotted his own, so there was nothing but the waiting precipice between the meeting of their flesh.

Their sexual interludes to this point had been flashes of fire. This was a slow, hot burn, his kisses upon her throat and lips taking an eternity until she was only sensation in his arms. She couldn't think past each place his mouth pressed and held, tasting her flesh with bare movements of his lips that rocketed through her nerve endings from the point of contact to her toes. She gripped her fingers in his hair, holding him to her, and realized her body was moving with a life of its own, her hips rising, circling, stroking against him in insistent demand.

He lifted his head, his body lying upon hers, his arms sliding up so his elbows were on either side of her shoulders, holding some of his weight off of her.

"How does this feel?" he asked, his fingertips doing a light stroke of her cheek, his eyes darkening as her head turned and she caught his finger in her mouth, biting him with sharp teeth. She curled her tongue around the imprisoned digit and let him withdraw it slowly, glistening with the moistness of her mouth. He groaned and caught her face in his hands, pressing his body down on hers to keep her still. "I need to know if you're okay. You're trembling."

"I'm not afraid. I want this. I want you." She reached up and touched his face, tracing his forehead, the slope of his nose, the curve of the bone under his eye. He brought his lips to the pulse point on her wrist, and she rested her hand on his face. Her blood pounded against his mouth. His cock moved against her, a bump of movement, and she felt wetness against her thigh, her wetness mixing with his. Something in that place between her legs was pulsing as hard as the blood through her wrist, and thousands of years of instinct told her what it wanted. It was an ache connected to the tightness in her chest, the trembling in her body. If this was merely lust, she could understand why it was so often confused with love, but she knew Conlon was right. Whatever this was, it was more than lust, even if it was too sudden to be called love.

Her hips rocked up, brushing her pussy against him, and he groaned against her wrist.

"Slow down, kitten," he muttered. "I don't want to rush this."

He moved down to her neck, and she arched her whole body, telegraphing the ancient female message of surrender and trust, that she was open to him, his to claim.

His arms curled under her waist, holding her in her arched position as he bit her neck then tortured it with his tongue, the rough afternoon shadow of his beard rasping against the pale skin over her breastbone. She could do little with her arms but let them lie on either side of her. All her energy seemed to be drawing toward one place. Her hips pressed up, circling, rubbing in a manner she could not stop, a continuing call to his body to come into hers, to bring her to that place that the magic, and now her own desires, demanded.

Instead of succumbing to her body's plea, he heightened it by sliding down her body and bringing his lips to her breast, nibbling the skin to her nipple and then covering it with the warm, sucking pressure of his mouth.

Now she did catch hold of him, her fingers gripping those massive shoulders. "Conlon," she said. He murmured, an incoherent noise of desire against her flesh.

She closed her eyes and suddenly the world turned over. She surfaced in the hot spring of Conlon's body and mind. The red heat of his desire rolled over her, through her. She felt the tightening of his body, preparing to take the woman beneath him, as clearly as if it were her own body. Her mind seesawed between shock and the muddled confusion of arousal. Her empathy had never received anything but negative emotions, emotions of darkness. This was a melding of two desires in a heated rush of sensation, and she felt both of them.

Her muddled mind tried to make sense of it. Perhaps as this physical act opened her mind, her empathy gave her the gift of being able to merge in this way with her lover. She had never done this before. Anything was possible.

It was a very plausible explanation, and her moment of fear turned into wonder and then a wild craving, for now she felt his desire as well as her own, and the demand was overwhelming. For the first time in her life, she experienced joy in her ability to experience what lay in the mind of another.

I feel it too. Marisa, I feel you. In my mind, in my body. In my heart.

She had a brief flash of his intense hazel eyes focused on her own before his mouth was on hers again, driving away any rational thought. His hand moved in between them, guiding himself to her.

He had brushed his cock against her as he suckled her

breast, but now his intentional navigation brought his broad head firmly against her moist lips. She had no fear of this. He had taken that away. Now she just wanted. She opened her legs wider and he murmured hot approval, biting at her lips as she answered with a soft cry of encouragement.

Her pussy stretched to take his head in, her thighs spreading and lifting. The warm wetness of her body eagerly welcomed him. The shaft of his cock followed, that impressive column of flesh and steel she could not get her fingers around. He was widening her but taking his time, moving in slowly, his fingers sliding up off his shaft once he had it inexorably in its track to gently pinch her clit, making her hips wiggle and move faster, her breath coming in pants at the sensation that spiraled through her in rhythm with the pump of her hips.

She felt the tremendous control he was exercising to hold back, and she didn't want that. She wanted him, all the way inside, now. Her hands slipped down, finding the slick muscles of his buttocks. She clutched him, lifting her hips as if she could impale herself.

"Jesus," he rasped, "hold on, kitten. I don't want to hurt you. You're such a little thing."

She did not listen, her clutch insistent. Her legs rose to fold over her hands on his buttocks, her muscles inadvertently squeezing, tightening on him in her channel. Being in his mind at the same time she was in her own, she knew how much he wanted to be inside her and exploited every image she could see through his mind's eye to try to make him surrender to her will.

He met the shield of her maidenhead and stopped, resisting her with his greater physical strength and a mental control she would have admired if she didn't want him so desperately.

"No turning back," he whispered, his face above her, framed by the soft light of a dying day. "Hold on, kitten, and trust me. Let yourself go."

He surged forward, breaking through her innocence in one sharp, clean movement, seating himself to the hilt in the same motion. Marisa cried out, but it was a short pain, one that could not detract from the overwhelming experience of having a man's body so deeply within her, so irrevocably connected to hers. It was an intimacy she had never had, always been afraid to hope for. In that one act of burying his cock in her, he had filled the empty place in her heart.

He whispered to her, the words not important. He held still, his powerful body trembling as he let her get accustomed to the feel of him, and then he pulled back. One inch, another inch, the thick shaft teasing her clit, the head stroking her inside. Then he came forward again, as if he was drawing a bow over the strings of an instrument, and her body tightened, rippling with the music he was creating.

"Oh," she breathed. "Oh."

He smiled then, a faint gesture as dream-like as the twilight air, and he did it again. And again. Just as slow each time, even though the fire burned exponentially hotter with each stroke, and her body screamed with the desire to push to full conflagration. He kept her smoldering, hotter, hotter, his teeth gritted, the tense muscles of his jaw giving his handsome face the appearance of smooth creek rock, slick with his sweat.

"You need the slowness, kitten," he rasped. "I know you want to go over, but you need an easy pace."

And she did. He was so large that her newly stretched muscles needed time to learn how to ease and tighten on him in a way that brought them both pleasure. So she trembled on that pinnacle and focused inside herself, marking the give of her muscles as he pushed inward, then their jealous squeezing as he pulled back, communicating her desire to hold onto him. It made her gasp with the mutual pleasure she gave them both. She found the rhythm, matched him stroke for stroke and felt the beat of their hearts, the pump of their lungs and the motion of their bodies become aligned.

"Trust me, Marisa," he repeated, his words lost in a groan of restraint. "Let go, kitten. Let go."

Why did he keep saying that when he would not let her get to that wonderful precipice of sensation? His hips changed their angle so that his thrusts rubbed a seesaw motion against the opening to her cunt, her clit, and a circle of pleasure inside that seemed no bigger than her pinkie print. Each rub of his head against it, and the stroke of his shaft out against the clit, drove her higher but not over.

As her arousal grew, her consciousness expanded as she had predicted but also much farther than she had anticipated. Beyond the room, beyond the clearing, it flung itself out like a roll of clouds, farther than it had ever been able to reach, into the nearby town and beyond. Marisa felt the height as if she was on top of a mountain, looking down on thousands of souls. As suddenly as she became aware of them, they became aware of her.

Her fingers clutched on his skin. "Conlon."

She tried to speak further, but she couldn't get the words out. He pressed his lips against her ear, and it felt as if his voice spoke from deep within her. "I'm here, kitten. Don't be afraid."

They were coming toward her from all directions, like a tidal wave from which there was no escape. She could not move, frozen in their sights as they descended upon her, shoving aside her shields, trampling them beyond repair, leaving her completely vulnerable.

Their darkest emotions poured over and into her like a flood of bright flashing lights, hurting and blinding her inner eye. Her body stiffened. That pinnacle of pleasure so close a moment before was now lost in the confusion, blasted away beyond her reach.

Use me, Marisa. Look. Use me. LOOK.

Conlon's voice was a roar in her head, a command that she thrashed around within herself to find. As she turned amidst all the light, she saw a point of blessed darkness. She fought toward it, her survival instinct shoving down her panic enough to make her focus on getting to it.

As she kept it within her sights, it grew larger, a dark vortex before her inner eye. The harsh lights surrounded it, but none penetrated that welcoming blackness. Her subconscious ran for that shelter, scrabbled for it, urged on by his voice in her head, calling her over and over.

Come to me, kitten. Come now.

She stumbled and fell into the darkness, wrapped its protection around herself like a cloak. As abruptly as she had been sucked under by fear and despair, she exploded back into her consciousness and gasped, gripped by spiraling strokes of pleasure in a dizzying wave of sensation, for Conlon was still moving within her.

Only now his movements were fierce and strong as he pulled her to him with the demands of his body and her own, breaking the power of the invading force over her will and desires.

Her body arched and all those complex nerve endings in her pussy began to vibrate, a warning, a promise of the strength of the magic sweeping over her. The climax struck with the power of a summer storm, rumbling out of the depths of the sky and earth, taking her over, opening her mouth in a scream she could not stop. It erupted from her, the force of her orgasm electrifying the lights gathered like hungry demons just beyond Conlon's protection and driving them back even further.

Conlon's hands tightened, a bruising but welcome grip on her body, and he let go, pouring hot seed into her. It shattered her emotional shields, her personal defenses against his impact on her emotions, the yearnings he had raised in her. Their bodies moved together as one, synchronized by mysteries that were centuries old.

In the amazing link their joining had forged, she could feel the limitless space within him for her spirit to turn and draw his essence around her. With that around her unprotected psyche, she could face the world she so often had to shut out. She sensed them, those many consciousnesses, but they could not attack her. They could not come within the circle of his protection without her permission. She could filter them. She felt the ones genuinely in need of healing, the good soul gone astray, and the ones who had willingly succumbed to the petty desires of the selfish heart. However, without the attack on her senses, the cacophony from the negative vibrations could be dimmed, and she could see how best to help, how to set any of them on a better path. Not just with her potions but with her empathic understanding of their needs.

She could not see him physically on this plane of awareness, but it was a place where emotion was more powerful than physical sense. He was there with her, his soul and mind, seeing what she was seeing, standing with her, lending his protection to her power. That was Conlon Maguire's gift, a limitless well of protective power to offer, fueled by his pure spirit and the accumulation of a life spent protecting others, a White Knight in truth.

When the powerful grip of the orgasm started to ease, like the ebbing tide of a sparkling ocean at sunset, something even more amazing happened. She saw all those flashing lights fade away, back to their respective souls, and yet she was still warmly ensconced in Conlon, their spirits intertwined like their bodies.

Yet it was no spirit but a human male under her fingertips, with sweaty, muscled skin pressed against the inside of her thighs. Who even now scratched her neck with his stubble as he nuzzled her, his heart thundering against hers. A real man who could answer the quiet desires of her woman's heart and stand by her for the life the Lord and Lady had given her.

The miracle Laraset had promised was in her arms. Her soulmate. Capable of giving her the strength and shielding to live the life she chose, not the life forced upon her to survive.

Marisa was so overcome she could not speak, and the shudders of her body were now fueled as much by her tears as the post-coital aftershocks of desire. Conlon did not speak for a long while. He simply held her, kissed away each tear. He let her see the knowledge in his eyes, the promise that had been there all along, that she had not recognized until the magic was released by their joining.

When the emotional and physical tumult had ebbed enough that she lay quiet in his arms, she spoke at last in a voice hoarse with emotion.

"Why didn't you tell me?" She held onto him as if he might vanish if she let him out of her body, and he tightened his hold around her, understanding her need.

"Why the potion?"

"I couldn't have told you, kitten. Something like this I had to show you, and I could only show you if you let it be more than sex. Your heart had to be open to the possibility of love between us, of forever. If you had closed down, only given me your body, it wouldn't have worked."

She ran the palms of her hands down the muscles of his broad back, arched with a sigh as his thighs tightened at her touch, driving him more deeply within her. "How did you find me?"

"It's been a thirty-two-year search." He smiled, rubbed his nose against the side of her face. "It ended when I went to a Sioux medicine man by the name of Kohana." He pulled back so he could face her surprised look. "I went there to do a sweat lodge after Peru. To heal."

Now it was her turn to press upward, put her cheek against his rough jaw, caress his ear and neck with her fingertips. His jaw moved against her skin.

"In my vision in the sweat lodge, I saw you clearly for the first time, but at that moment, I knew you had always been there, in me. Like that moment when you find your destiny and you think, 'ah, there you are'. You were it for me, kitten.

"No, no more tears." He raised a lock of her hair, pressed it to the corner of her eye. "Imagine my joy at having a vision of you when I'd been locked in a sweat lodge for three days with a bunch of other unwashed guys." She managed a smile and he used his lips to catch the next tear that fell. "There you were among us," he said. "But I was the only one who could see you. You were like Snow White. Ruby red lips, pale, perfect skin, raven hair falling forward over ripe breasts cradled in lace and velvet. I wanted you so much that from that moment forward you were a constant ache in my heart and my cock." He wound his fingers around her hair, tightening his hold. "From the first moment I saw you in my dreams I wanted to spread your legs and make you mine."

He kissed her neck, bit. Marisa trembled in his arms, aroused and overcome by his words, but he showed no mercy, taking her from laughter to tears to passion to joy.

"I wanted to curl my arms around you, shield every part of your body and soul with the strength of mine, reassure you, be your lover and your friend, be everything you needed, forever. Your shadow was already printed on my soul. I wanted the real thing in my arms."

He lifted his head, their eyes less than a finger width apart. "I told Kohana all I saw and he said, 'This woman is your calling, your true destiny and your lifemate. I will tell you how to find her, but winning her will not be easy. You will have to approach as the true hunter who respects and reveres his prey must. With strategy and stealth.'" Humor flitted through his eyes at that, reflected in her own, as Marisa could well imagine the eccentric Kohana laughing at them both.

"He told me to go halfway across the country, to this tiny hole-in-the-wall town, and find an old woman living in the woods on its outskirts. This woman, he told me, would be the key to finding my soulmate. It was the only warning he gave me. He didn't tell me I'd find you here. It took everything I could do not to fall down at your feet and beg when I first saw your face."

Marisa smiled. "Strategy and stealth." She cocked her brow, bit her lip when he shifted within her. "Well, Mr. Maguire, you did a very good job with both." She placed her hands on his face, held him there so she could stare at him, this miracle that she didn't quite believe wasn't a dream. "With you, I felt what people were feeling," she said, "but I could control it. I could pick and choose, and I could feel the bad *and* the good, not just the bad. It's like I always could, but the volume knob on the bad was just turned up so high it drowned the good out." She blinked more tears from her eyes and he smiled, kissing them away again.

"I know. I felt it when you turned it down, took control. It was marvelous, kitten."

With a groan she found endearing and amusing, he rolled off her, taking her with him so she lay on his chest. "We don't have to be joined physically to do that. Laraset and Kohana told me if we made it work, we'd eventually be able to link spiritually and I'll be able to protect you, even if we're not together. Like if one of us is traveling, or at the grocery store," he added, seeing her sudden look of apprehension. He reached up, touched her cheek. "You can go anywhere, kitten, anywhere you want to go. Though I'll admit, I kind of like doing it the physical way."

She found a tiny smile, her worries easing. His large hand cupped her face. "Forever, Marisa," he said quietly. Firmly. "I'll talk you into falling in love with me. I might even confuse you enough to get you to marry me in a weak moment. Maybe have my child."

He looked at her steadily, waited for her reaction. Marisa swallowed down a lifetime of fear and chose to believe in miracles again, accept his reality.

"Yes," she said.

His eyes darkened and he raised up on his elbow, taking her down to her back to kiss her, long and hard, curling his arms under her to pull her up against his body. When he lifted his head, he kept her tight within his embrace. Her arms were folded against his chest, between the two of them like a pair of delicate bird wings, and her fingers fanned out on his collarbone, touching him.

"I'm scared though," she admitted. "The idea of children."

The corner of his mouth lifted. "That's the thing you can fear least, kitten. When I had my vision in the sweat lodge, I saw you in three images. First, I saw the face of the old lady, your illusion. The Crone face, Kohana called her. Then I saw the raven-haired beauty, as I said. The Maiden. But my soul knew neither of these was the true face of the woman I loved. It was when you appeared to me as a Mother, I knew I was seeing your true self. The mother of my child," he shifted, laid her hand on her stomach, "a child we may have just planted in your body."

Marisa felt a thrill flutter through her as he laid his hand on hers. He stroked her knuckles, traced the delicate skin of her bare stomach in the open spaces between her fingers. "But more than that, you're a Mother in the sense of capital M. A Mother and healer to the souls of many, as many as your generous heart and what you call the Lord and Lady will bring to you."

She turned her hand, linked it with his and wiggled around so she was lying on her side, facing him. Her mind could not digest the enormity of it all so she chose to focus on a random thought niggling at the edge of her mind. "So, that butterfly thing. That was part of your strategy?"

He grinned at her, stretched his free arm over his head. "Never know what methods you'll need to convince a woman to see your point of view. It worked, didn't it?"

"Ooh, you..." she scrambled, snatched the spoon off the floor and went after him with it. They wrestled in the bed a moment or two, him laughing until he got it away from her and set her on his loins, seating his cock firmly against her. She quieted like a child given a pacifier, her hands braced on his solid chest, feeling the beat of his heart as he lay beneath her.

"Eventually," he said, "we'll go see your parents."

"Oh, Conlon, I don't know."

"Kitten, if your mother and father got the chance to hold you in their arms once without causing you pain, it would do more to bring healing and closure to their lives than a thousand of your letters, no matter how well written they are. You've got adopted siblings out there. They deserve to know you."

She shook her head. "But I don't know—"

"There's no rush on anything, Marisa. None. We have time. We definitely have tonight," he smiled, a slow, sexy gesture that made her stomach somersault, "and I'm in no hurry to leave a bed with you in it. You remember me talking about those threads? They'll guide us, and they're strong. They'll bear us up no matter where we go, even if we decide to spin all our dreams from here. Fate finds us anywhere. All you have to do now is think about tonight." His fingers eased down her spine and his gaze descended as well, considering her naked body. He cupped her breasts, brushed the tips of her nipples with his thumbs. "I'm thinking—"

"Conlon, you couldn't." She felt him hardening beneath her pussy and her gaze flitted to his intent one. "Or I could be wrong."

"Any objections?"

A smile crept onto her face, its light coming from her heart and the growing warmth of her own body. "I hope those are REALLY strong threads," she said as he banded his arms around her, bringing her body down fully on top of his. "Because if we spin them from this bed, I don't know of a potion strong enough to hold up the frame."

"I do," he murmured, bringing her breast down to his eager mouth. "Let me show you how to make it."

The End

READY FOR MORE?

Check out Joey's website at storywitch.com where you'll find additional information, free excerpts, buy links and news about current and upcoming releases for all of her books and series.

You can find free vignettes and friends to share them with at the JWH Connection, a Joey W. Hill fan forum created by and operated for fans of Joey W. Hill. Sign up instructions are available at storywitch.com/community.

Finally, be sure to check out the latest newsletter for information on upcoming releases, book signing events, contests, and more. You can view current and past editions and subscribe to receive upcoming editions at storywitch.com/community or click the link under the Community menu.

About the Author

Joey W. Hill writes about vampires, mermaids, boardroom executives, cops, witches, angels, housemaids... She's penned over forty acclaimed titles and six award-winning series, and been awarded the RT Book Reviews Career Achievement Award for Erotica. But she's especially proud and humbled to have the support and enthusiasm of a wonderful, widely diverse readership.

So why erotic romance? "Writing great erotic romance is all about exploring the true face of who we are – the best and worst - which typically comes out in the most vulnerable moments of sexual intimacy." She has earned a reputation for writing BDSM romance that not only wins her fans of that genre, but readers who would "never" read BDSM romance. She believes that's because strong, compelling characters are the most important part of her books.

"Whatever genre you're writing, if the characters are captivating and sympathetic, the readers are going to want to see what happens to them. That was the defining element of the romances I loved most and which shaped my own writing. Bringing characters together who have numerous emotional obstacles standing in their way, watching them reach a soul-deep understanding of one another through the expression of their darkest sexual needs, and then growing from that understanding into love - that's the kind of story I love to write."

Take the plunge with her, and don't hesitate to let her know what you think of her work, good or bad. She thrives on feedback!

Find more of her work by following her on Facebook and Twitter, and check out her website for more books by Joey W. Hill.

Twitter: @JoeyWHill

Facebook: JoeyWHillAuthor

On the Web: www.storywitch.com

Email: storywitch@storywitch.com

Also by Joey W. Hill

Arcane Shot Series

Something About Witches
In the Company of Witches

Daughters of Arianne Series

A Mermaid's Kiss
A Witch's Beauty
A Mermaid's Ransom

Knights of the Board Room Series

Board Resolution
Controlled Response
Honor Bound
Afterlife
Hostile Takeover
Willing Sacrifice
Soul Rest

Nature of Desire Series

Holding the Cards
Natural Law

Ice Queen
Mirror of My Soul
Mistress of Redemption
Rough Canvas
Branded Sanctuary
Divine Solace

Naughty Bits Series

The Lingerie Shop
Training Session
Bound To Please
The Highest Bid

Naughty Wishes Series

Part 1: Body
Part 2: Heart
Part 3: Mind
Part 4: Soul

Vampire Queen Series

Vampire Queen's Servant
Mark of the Vampire Queen
Vampire's Claim
Beloved Vampire
Vampire Mistress
Vampire Trinity
Vampire Instinct
Bound by the Vampire Queen
Taken by a Vampire
The Scientific Method

Nightfall

Elusive Hero

Night's Templar

Non-Series Titles

If Wishes Were Horses

Virtual Reality

Unrestrained

Novellas

Chance of a Lifetime

Choice of Masters

Make Her Dreams Come True

Threads of Faith

Submissive Angel

Short

Snow Angel